"Do you believe in fate?"

Rennie asked, her v

John emitted a long, holding trapped in hi Indians believe that it ...... you do with your life that determines your fate."

She moistened her lips and tilted her face up to him. "And what do the Seminoles say about two people coming together for only one night? Would they call that fate?"

His whole body tensed. "They would say that a man and a woman coming together can change the course of the world, and must not be taken lightly."

"I don't want to change the whole world. Only my world."

"I don't want to hurt you," he whispered. "You're vulnerable right now, and confused. You don't know what you really want."

Her hands came up to caress his face. "For the first time in my life, I know *exactly* what I want."

Panther on
the Prowl
NANCY MORSE

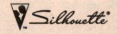

INTIMATE MOMENTS™

Published by Silhouette Books

America's Publisher of Contemporary Romance

Books by Nancy Morse

Silhouette Intimate Moments

Sacred Places #181
Run Wild, Run Free #210
The Mom Who Came To Stay #683
A Child of His Own #773
Panther on the Prowl #1134

NANCY MORSE

Nancy lives in New York and Florida with her husband, Talley, who works in the film industry, and their Alaskan Malamute, Max, aka Big Fur. An early love of reading and happy endings led to the publication of her first historical romance in 1980. She has an avid interest in Native American art and culture and takes pride in her collection of nineteenth-century artifacts. In addition to writing, she keep busy with reading, gardening, aerobic workouts and a full-time job in health and education.

Chapter 1

Rennie Hollander was desperate.

The practiced hands at the controls trembled and her usually steady grip was scared and unsure as she piloted the single-engine Cessna southward, hugging the Florida coastline.

All around, lightning snaked the black sky. The sudden, violent thunderstorm that ripped through the night shortly after takeoff should have forced her to turn around and head back to Palm Beach International, but the radio frequencies were flooded with diverted pilots trying to talk to tower controllers. And besides, it would have been a mistake to go back.

Fixing her coordinates, she flew on into the thick night. The steady hum of the engine was the only

In the years following her mother's marriage to the senator, the conflict within her deepened. Hers was the kind of life that most people only dreamed about, with private flying lessons, the best schools, summers in Southampton, winters in Palm Beach. But like the vast wetland somewhere down there in the darkness beyond the plane's window, Rennie felt empty and alone. Something was missing. She referred to it as her missing link.

The family wealth notwithstanding, Rennie preferred to earn her own living as a professor of anthropology with the University of Miami. Her work gave her life some focus. She didn't earn much, but at least she earned it herself. Besides, there was always the trust fund to fall back on. Not that she needed it. She already had everything she could want—except, of course the things that really mattered, like the love she lost when her father died and the attention she rarely received from a mother who had been too busy hosting lavish parties and fund-raising events for her husband.

Growing up, money had always been the only constant thing in her life. The more she had of it, the less she needed of everything else. But as she grew older, what was once difficult for a little girl to understand became frighteningly clear to the woman she had become. Where was the desire? The need? The sheer necessity for life? That old missing link churned deep inside, filling her with the need to need something...someone.

There was a horrible noise, followed in less than a heartbeat by a jolt that pitched Rennie forward in her seat. A ferocious heat welled up behind her. She didn't have to turn around to know that the plane was on fire and that she was going to crash.

There was a bone-shattering thud when the plane hit the ground. Cushioned by the soft, damp earth, it remained in one piece. Rennie was shaken violently from side to side as the tail section spun around and around, churning over the muck and saw grass.

When the plane finally came to a stop, Rennie found herself miraculously alive and pinned beneath the wreckage. Jet fuel from the engine poured on her. Her fingers clawed at the seat belt. In her frenzy she got it unbuckled. Disentangling herself from the wreckage, she fell out of the plane into the swamp.

Worse than the awful sound of the crash was the crushing silence that greeted her. There was no noise, no movement, no life, it seemed in the cold, raw darkness that swallowed her up. She stumbled away from the plane, mindless of injuries and fearful of the sinister creatures that lurked in the swamp. Alligators came to mind. Snakes. And panthers. God only knew what was out there. It was so dark she couldn't see a thing. Then a startling realization came over her. The darkness all around her was not caused by the veil of night or because her eyes were shut. Her eyes were, in fact, wide open. She blinked several times just to make sure. Yes, open. Her

it was the only reason he was marrying her. It had all been a charade—their first meeting, the court-ship, everything had been carefully orchestrated by Craig to get the land.

She thought that marrying Craig was a way to test her independence and find some shelter from the influence of her family, but his betrayal only proved that she hadn't been making the right choices for herself. Why hadn't she seen it before? Maybe she just hadn't wanted to see. Maybe she'd been uncon-sciously trying to replace the father she lost at an early age. Whatever the reason, the eye-opening ex-perience drove home the realization of just how im-portant it was for her to stand on her own two feet and not to depend on someone else for happiness, especially someone as controlling as Craig.

Rennie struggled to awaken, but unconsciousness maintained its tenacious hold, and all she could do was thrash this way and that in a vain attempt to block out the images.

The images faded and returned and faded again until, in the end, she sank even deeper, to a place where there were no memories or images, only a nothingness in which to take refuge.

It could have been minutes, hours or days before she crawled painfully awake out of unconsciousness. There came to her the smell of the damp earth. It seemed somehow familiar, but her mind was hung with moss and cobwebs and was unable to make a connection.

It went on like that until something called her away from the darkness and back to the conscious world. It was the touch of hands working with amazing gentleness to peel the dressing away, hands of mercy applying a soothing compress to the burned skin around her eyes, followed by fresh gauze.

Her voice, unsure and untested, scratched painfully at the back of her throat and emerged as a husky whisper. "Am I in a hospital?"

"No."

The singular word uttered in a deep pitch that was both unfamiliar and unfriendly made her shudder.

"Wh-where am I?"

"You're at my place."

There was no mistaking the inhospitable edge to the voice that spoke, conflicting sharply with the tenderness of the hands that applied fresh gauze to her eyes.

There was a scent about him, of the forest and the damp soil, a scent that Rennie found both comforting for the mother-earth images it conjured up, and frightening with visages of wild things.

She could feel his presence in the very air she breathed, and she wondered how it was possible to be so aware of a man she could not even see.

She drew back, partly out of caution—she had no idea who he was—but mostly from the unanticipated warmth that began at the tips of her fingers and spread clear down to her toes. Appalled at such a

Rennie's mind struggled to assimilate the information it was receiving and make some sense out of it. Everglades? Plants and herbs? A name like Panther? "What are you?" she asked. "An Indian?"

He answered stoically, "Seminole, to be precise."

That would explain the essence of something wild that she felt about him, but what was the reason for that inhospitable tone of voice? She sank down onto the mattress...his mattress...his bed. She could smell it now, the scent of the Everglades, the scent of him, lingering on the pillow as her head fell back onto it.

She was scarcely aware of his footsteps retreating to the opposite side of the room, or of the quiet stirrings of his movements as he went about doing whatever it was he was doing. Within minutes he returned. The edge of the bed sank from his weight when he sat down beside her.

"Here. Drink this."

His hand moved to the back of her head, strong fingers entwining in her hair as he lifted her head and urged a cup to her lips.

Rennie sipped the hot liquid that tasted like tree bark and dirt, and wrinkled her nose. "What are you trying to do, poison me?"

"It's just an infusion of valerian root to calm you and some local plants to help ease the pain."

In no time the raw pain around her eyes began to

press her to reveal her last name. She'd never been a very good liar, and loathed the thought of having to make one up. His motive for helping her might be different if he knew that she came from a wealthy family, so she reasoned that it was better if he didn't know who she was and what she was running from.

"Is there anyone I can contact for you?"

"No." She spoke a little too quickly. Forcing a calm into her voice that she did not feel, she explained, "There's no one. My parents are deceased, and I have no brothers or sisters."

It was true, of course. Her impervious mother died a few years ago, her beloved father when she was young enough to feel the impact for the rest of her life, and she was an only child. Nevertheless, she felt as guilty as if she had blatantly lied to him.

Skirting the evasion, she ventured to ask, "Do you know how long it will take for my eyes to heal?"

"The skin around them will heal in a few weeks. As for your sight…only time will tell."

"Am I…blind?"

"I had a doctor come by to examine you. He's a Seminole healer from Big Cypress who's also a licensed physician. He says your blindness is caused by a swelling of the optic nerve. In most cases the swelling eventually subsides and sight is restored."

Rennie sucked in her breath at his brutal honesty.

"Would you rather I lie to you?" he asked.

No, not another lie. She didn't think she could

her own lost past, the one that ended with the death of her father. She never expected that she would come to love her work as much as she did, nor that her struggle to reconcile her past would lead her to this place.

"You've got to stay somewhere," he said.

But for Rennie it wasn't that simple. It had been easy for her to think that Craig was the answer to her self-sufficiency. Easy to imagine herself happily married to a man she now knew would have been as controlling as the senator. Easy to see her mistakes when, because of her blindness, she was unable to see anything else. For now, however, she was grateful for the gauze that sealed her sight, for despite John Panther's unfriendly tone, she felt safe in his care.

"Couldn't I stay here?"

She knew by the palpable silence that filled the room that he didn't like the idea. Inwardly she cringed. Where had she gotten the nerve to ask such a thing? But desperate problems called for desperate solutions and brought out a certain recklessness she didn't know she had when next she said, "I could pay you."

He answered with wry annoyance, "With what? Whatever money you had with you is buried beneath the wreckage."

Another man might have asked how much, and then been slack-jawed when she named a ridiculously high figure. She was no longer afraid to hide

"I'm a biologist with the Everglades Research Center."

"What do you research?" She was desperately tired and struggling to stay awake, but a part of her wanted to know...needed to know...more about the man in whose care she was entrusting herself. He could have been an ax murderer, for all she knew. But there was nothing sinister in the air around him, no hint of danger or violence. And except for that unsettling scent that hovered about him, of something wild and unforgiving, she felt no menace from him.

"I study the ecosystem of the swamp and monitor the animal population."

"At night?" she questioned.

"There are creatures that live in the swamp that come out only at night."

"Creatures?"

"Don't worry. They won't bother you here."

Rennie didn't share his confidence. "Are we near anything? A town or a village?"

"There's nothing for miles."

That would account for the acute loneliness that seemed to pervade every corner of the room. The secluded place, made even more secret by her sightlessness, made Rennie feel lost.

"You live here all by yourself?"

"Yes."

The deep, single-word reply made her shiver. What kind of man shunned the company of others,

frightened. For one thing she was feeling far too light-headed to entertain any dangerous notions about him. For another, even in her muddled state something told her that beneath the annoyance and unfriendly tone beat the heart of a kind man. Why would he bother to help her if he were not good-hearted? The undercurrent of wildness she had initially perceived about him must have been the workings of a weak and vulnerable imagination.

The protective arms of sleep wrapped around her, drawing her to its breast as it whispered words of gentle comfort into her ear. She tried hard to concentrate on what it was saying and was surprised to find that it wasn't words at all. It was a sound, an easy shhh somewhere beyond these walls.

In a small voice that hovered midway between conscious thought and dream, she breathed, "That sound. What's that sound?"

"That's the saw grass," he said. "A river of grass swaying in the breeze." His voice was low with reflection from across the room. "Sometimes I can sit and listen to it for hours. If you wade into it and look down, you can see the water moving slowly, almost imperceptibly, past your feet. So gradually it makes you wonder whether we move through life or life moves past us."

But Rennie wasn't listening. She was asleep, lulled into slumber by the effect of the tea, the shhh of the saw grass, and John Panther's hypnotic, regretful voice.

He loved this place like no other. The soft, squishy land, the creatures that lived in the mangrove forests and swam in the still, shallow water, the grass, as sharp as saw blades, swaying hypnotically in the breeze, the sky, so endless and unfettered there was room for a whole month of sunsets in a single evening such as this.

If the mosquitoes had not been so thick and the land so soggy, the white men who came here would have split the mahogany hammocks for lumber and turned the mangrove forests into fertilizer and cattle feed long ago. Resort hotels would now stud the wild beaches. The land he loved would have been drained and subdivided and carved into lots, and he would not be standing here now looking out at its ferocious beauty with as much awe as if he were seeing it for the very first time.

The land itself was as flat as a Kansas wheatfield, but what to some was monotonous, John found hypnotic. It was what drew him to the window at just about this time each day, when it was neither light nor dark, when the world seemed to hover in a sort of limbo where there was no past to haunt him and no future to look forward to, when the sky was ablaze with color and all that mattered was the moment and the land. This was country that had to be understood. It was a wild, unforgiving place inhabited by dangerous, venomous creatures. And the most dangerous of all was the one that looked back at him in the clear glass.

a sense of his own place in the world and an acceptance of and reverence for the things around him. Being a loner at heart only added to the stereotyping and had made not dating easy. Until Maggie.

Maggie laughed at the white world's idea of what it was to be Indian. She knew there was nothing savage about him. These days, whatever fierceness he possessed was born out of tragedy, the kind that wounds so deeply it turns a soft heart into a hard one. He wondered if Maggie would even recognize him now.

He never asked her to give up her dream of going to San Francisco. She did so willingly. And together they planned a new dream for the future. She continued to wait tables while he studied for his master's degree. When he landed a job with the Everglades Research Center, she quit her job at the luncheonette to concentrate on painting and sculpting.

Having been born in a chickee made of cypress wood and palmetto leaves, like most of his people, John didn't expect much from a world that was decidedly white and hostile. But a hundred years of white influence could not eradicate the one thing he was above all else. Seminole. In his Indian soul he had no wish to be any different or better than he was. He merely wished to be. Working in his own backyard among the creatures and cattails of the swamp, returning home to the reservation each night to be with his wife, was more than he could ever

warrior didn't say a prayer to the Spirit Being for taking the life of one of its children. Angered, the Spirit Being condemned the warrior to wander the earth for all time by day as a man, by night as a panther.

The legend struck a particularly painful chord inside of John. Could it be that the panther he'd been hunting was the one the old ones spoke of? That would explain the clever way the beast eluded him. Some would say he was crazy to even think it, but deep in his Seminole heart, John wasn't so sure. His curiosity was almost as great as his thirst for vengeance. But if myths and legends were supposed to teach us about ourselves, what was it teaching him about himself? Could it be that he was doomed by fate to follow the same crazy path as the legend, wandering around by day emotionally cut off from the rest of the world, at night adrift in his grief and alone? If there was any lesson to be learned from it all, it had to do with the part he played in a cycle of vengeance begun by some ancient warrior and which lived on inside of him.

Why couldn't he have left the panther alone instead of tracking it relentlessly? Was it the panther that caused Maggie's death, or was it really he himself for tampering with a greater plan and not leaving well enough alone? A year and a half later the questions remained unanswered. All that was left was the guilt, and an overriding vengeance for the panther. Yet as much as he hated the panther, that

skin, paled by her ordeal, glowed iridescently. Her sightless blue eyes had beamed out blinding quantities of light when he had applied fresh bandages, taking his breath away unexpectedly.

Her clothes were torn and scorched, but obviously expensive. Her hands were smooth-skinned and soft, bearing none of the calluses that scarred the palms of hardworking Seminole women. Her voice, weakened by the trauma and lulled by the infusion he'd given her, sounded different from any voice he'd ever heard. In it he could hear the culture and refinement that told him she was from a world very different from his.

She was running away from something, of that he was certain. But he wouldn't press her to reveal what it was. Who knew better than he did what it was like to run from something? He could not help but wonder as he watched her sleep how safe she would feel in his care if she knew that he had not been able to keep Maggie safe and the awful shame he carried over it.

Growing up in the company of alligators and ospreys did little to prepare John for the unexpected and unwelcome company of a pampered socialite, which seemed to be what she was. Hell, he didn't know anyone who flew their own plane. Again he reproached himself for the weakness in him that had him agreeing to let her stay. He hadn't known he possessed such weakness, having worked so hard to harden his heart, until she'd asked, and he'd looked

involved, which was really a laugh considering that he was in it up to his eyeballs.

John left his place by the window and crossed the room, his feet brushing the cypress planks with a noiselessness that came from years of tracking animals through the swamp. For many long moments he stared down at her. The brew he had given her would make her sleep through the night. Beyond the window some voiceless thing beckoned to him. *Come. Hurry. The moon rises and it's time to go hunting.* If he left now, he would be back by sunrise and she would never know the difference.

But he didn't move, not while there was still a sliver of daylight left and it fell so bewitchingly upon her face. Not while he was caught up in remembering what it was like to hold a woman's soft body in his arms and feel her breath against his neck.

For just that moment the memory did not hurt. Instead, it gave him a feeling of undisciplined delight just to feel it again and to realize that he was human after all.

had gone all cold and distant, and it was impossible to tell what he'd been thinking. In the next moment the chilling expression was gone, replaced by a smile friendly enough to charm a cobra. He'd asked her out for another night, making it clear that he would not take no for an answer.

She should have gotten an idea then of the lengths he would go to, to get what he wanted. A successful land developer like Craig Wolfson didn't get where he was by letting opportunities slip by. At the time she was flattered to think that what he wanted was her.

He liked to boast that one of the advantages of being rich was possessing things that most people could not, like the expensive and illegal Cuban cigar he extracted from a silver-inlaid case and placed between his lips as he spoke. Even now, as she lay upon John Panther's bed in the middle of the Everglades, her nose wrinkled at the awful smell of the cigar, and she shivered at the words that had been delivered like a slap across her face.

But as she had stood in the doorway, her shock turned slowly to outrage, and then to anger, raw and hot. She stormed into the room, her face white with fury, and broke off the engagement. She had no memory of taking the private elevator downstairs to the lobby, or of the doorman who held the door for her and wished her a good evening. All she could think about was the cold certainty with which he

for Rennie there was no light beyond the swath of bandages. Locked in her blindness, the awful memories seemed only that much more real.

The powerful effect of the infusion that John gave her last night had worn off sometime before daybreak. But now, no longer lulled into a state of painlessness, she was acutely aware of every ache in every muscle. Even the mere act of breathing hurt.

"Can I get you more tea?"

She didn't know he was there until he spoke in that deep, regretful voice. The air in the room was suddenly filled with him. How long had he been there, waiting in silence for her to surface? Could he read her thoughts as easily as he read her pain?

She turned her head toward him. In a ragged, untested voice, she said, "Maybe later. What time is it?"

"A little past three. Are you hungry?"

"I'd forgotten there was any such thing as food."

"You should eat something if you want more tea later. That infusion can be rough on an empty stomach. Yesterday you were too out of it to notice."

Rennie struggled to recall yesterday. God only knew how utterly pitiful she must have seemed to him. Too embarrassed to ask what she might have done or said, she stammered, "Was I— Did I—"

"You didn't reveal anything I shouldn't know. So...do you want some soup? I have chicken noodle, tomato and minestrone."

He forced the cylinder of soup from the can into a saucepan. "Is there?"

"Yes. But I'm afraid my cell phone is buried beneath the wreckage. Do you have a telephone I can use?"

The spoon clicked against the sides of the pot as John stirred the soup. "What sort of work do you do?"

"I'm a professor of anthropology."

"Sometimes," he said, "the farther we get from civilization, the more civilized we feel. Out here you'll find no e-mail, no voice messaging. Just an endless stream of rushing water to answer to. But I do have a cell phone for emergencies. I'll get it." He turned the soup to a slow simmer and went to get the phone. "Here you go." He touched the phone to her hand and stepped away.

The tonal beeps came slowly as Rennie felt her way across the keypad as she dialed the senator's private number.

"Hi, it's me. I know I should have called sooner, but I've been busy. Actually, I decided to take some time off. I'm staying with a friend. You can't reach me, but I'll be in touch." She hung up, feeling guilty for the evasion, but at least he would know that she was all right without knowing where she was.

"Out here you may not need one, but thank goodness for the answering machine." She handed the phone back to him. "Thank you, John."

He liked the way his name rolled off her tongue

"I'm assuming you can open a can of soup or boil water for spaghetti. That's all you'll find."

"I'm good at spaghetti. In college I lived on it. It's inexpensive and filling."

"You don't strike me as the type who's had to live on a budget."

Rennie wasn't surprised that he knew she was well off. She had practically admitted it only a few minutes ago when she had spoken without thinking. Still, what did he know about her reasons for preferring to make her own way rather than live off her family's wealth, or how her one stab at independence had not come without a price? Annoyance surfaced in her tone.

"Why? Because you think I can afford more? Didn't you say something about preconceived notions?"

John didn't like having his own words echoed back at him like that. "I don't judge people on what I see. I leave that to the hypocrites of the world. But there was nothing preconceived about that Cessna you were flying. You didn't earn the money for that on a professor's salary."

"That's true," she said. "I tapped into the trust fund my father set up for me before he died." She tilted her head up at him. "I owe no one an explanation or an apology for my background. The only person I owe that to is myself. So, I take it you've seen the wreckage?"

"I went to have a look at it this morning. It's

He questioned whether she could ever accept what he had done with no questions asked.

"I have to go out in a while. I'll ask Willie Cypress to look in on you. He's the one who found you. He can be trusted not to tell anyone you're here."

In the brief time Rennie had been with him, she had come to crave his company, what little there was of it and however reluctant he was to give it to her. Eagerly she asked, "When will you be back?"

"Daybreak."

"Oh."

Was that disappointment he heard in her voice? He told himself that she was either just lonely or afraid of the dark and that it had nothing to do with him.

"I go out every night," he said uncomfortably. "I told you that."

"Do you have to go just yet?"

He glanced toward the window. In a few hours it would be dark, and an aching voice would call to him from the swamp, beckoning to that dark place inside of him, and he would be powerless to resist it. But for now the sky was still light and the lurid urges that haunted him at sunset were at rest. He felt himself waver.

"Maybe I can stay a little longer."

across the room allowing her to get her bearings as she followed with her hand tucked in his. At the door he eased her forward and placed her fingers around the knob.

Rennie opened the door to a warm spring day. Standing in the doorway, she drew into her lungs deep breaths of air that was sweetly scented by an early-morning shower. The sunlight felt soothing upon her face, its warmth like a tonic to her bruised muscles and aching sensibilities. She took a cautious step outside and was silent for several moments. Finally she said, "This place must be very beautiful."

John glanced at her with surprise. "What makes you say that?"

"Because anything that feels this beautiful must be. Tell me what's out there. What does it look like?"

He looked skyward at the turkey vultures that carved arcs in the sky, and around them to the broad channel that ran past the cabin, monotonously bordered by mangroves. To the untrained eye they were surrounded by a million acres of soggy plants. It was hard to convince anyone of miracles in the absence of any visible evidence. But then, to find the miracles you had to have lived there all your life and have known where to look.

He came to stand beside her. For the first time he noticed that her head came just to the top of his shoulder. A breeze captured one golden strand of her hair and tossed it about in front of her eyes. Eyes

"It was pretty much the same for me," she said, "feeling apart because of your background. I chose a local college rather than the Ivy League school my family wanted me to attend because I thought that being around regular, working-class people would help me forget that I wasn't one of them."

"Did it work?"

She gave just a little smile, partly because of the irony and partly because it hurt to smile too broadly. "What do you think?"

"I think that no matter how hard you try, you can never get away from yourself." It was something he had learned in the past eighteen months, but if he told her that, he'd have to tell her the rest. He didn't want to think about it, and yet he couldn't think of anything else.

"The tribal council donated the money for my tuition. At that time I was one of the few of my people to even go to college, so I felt it was my duty to make them proud of me."

"Duty," she repeated dispassionately. Yes, she knew all about duty. Duty to a mother who married both times strictly for money and who tried to convince her to do the same. And duty to a stepfather who insisted that marriage to Craig Wolfson was the best thing for her. Maybe that was her problem: believing someone else always knew what was best for her.

"It's a funny thing about duty," she muttered.

the coontie plant, how to clear brush for a garden, to gather palmetto fronds for thatching, to pole a dugout canoe, to hunt deer. Whatever I needed to know as a Seminole she taught me.''

''And your father?''

He replied matter-of-factly, ''He ran out on us when we were kids.''

''And here I thought I had it rough when my father died when I was eight. At least he didn't leave on purpose.''

''I don't blame my father,'' said John. ''Not anymore. He's like the rest of us. We can't help being who we are. He was the restless kind who tried his hand at a lot of things. Beekeeping, trapping, cane grinding, running an airboat, gambling. There was always a poker game going in the back room when I was a kid. But I guess the thing he was best at was roaming.''

There was a faint fondness in his tone that children and grown-ups alike often have for a parent who has forsaken them, a love that suffers countless disappointments yet never quite goes away. To hear him speak about the father who deserted him, she realized that his feelings were no different from hers for the father who had died, and it made her feel a special kinship with him despite their differences.

''Why aren't you raising cattle like your brother?''

Solemnly he said, ''I guess you could say it's my destiny to be here.''

not wait for it to fall across the land. All the wild things of the night could not be as dangerous to him as this slender, tawny-haired woman was right now. Sure, they liked the same kind of soup. And okay, so maybe the loneliness they each experienced at college was not so very different. And losing a father was always tough under any circumstance. All right, so for some crazy reason they had these things in common. It didn't mean she would understand the part he played in Maggie's death and not hate him for it as much as he hated himself. Where would he even begin to tell her about it?

"John?"

Her soft voice called him away from the window and his tortured thoughts. "I heard you. I was just wondering where to begin."

"Why don't we start with the kitchen?"

There was no way to avoid taking her hand again and feeling her heat as he guided her through the doorway into the kitchen. He took her slowly around the small room, waiting patiently as her hands moved tentatively and then grew more confident as they explored the refrigerator, the stove, the sink, the cabinets.

"Soup," he explained, when she examined the cans in the cabinet. "It shouldn't be hard to remember that tomato is on the left, chicken noodle's in the middle and minestrone is on the right."

Disheartened, she said, "My life has been reduced to right and left."

the counter on either side of her. She could feel his arms coming to rest a hairbreadth from her body, which had gone all rigid.

"Turn around."

The plea in his voice made Rennie catch her breath. She was confused and afraid. It was one thing to fantasize about him, but quite another to actually give in to this crazy attraction she felt for a man she couldn't see.

"It's not what you think," he said. "I want to say something to you, and even if you can't see me, I want to say it to your face. Turn around." His tone was demanding, the plea slightly more urgent than before.

Rennie turned slowly around, brushing against his arms that did not withdraw until she was facing him. She knew that his eyes were upon her and felt herself melting from their heat.

"Please understand," he said. "I would have taken you in even if you weren't as beautiful as you are. And as far as telling no one that you're here, I'll respect that. But don't expect anything more from me. The fact is, I'm going to stay as far away from you as I can get. Believe me when I say it's for the best."

Rennie was aghast. "If you're assuming that I want more from you than a place to stay, you're mistaken."

"All I'm saying is, the imagination can play pow-

How was it possible to feel such attraction to a man she couldn't see, or to feel a longing for a man she had known for only a brief time? It had to be that she was feeling lonely and vulnerable in the aftermath of her experience with Craig.

"I'm tired," she said. "I'd like to lie down."

She made her way out of the kitchen on her own. With her hands outstretched before her, she groped her way back to the bed and sank down onto the soft mattress.

John let her go without offering assistance. She was right, it was his problem. He had created it a year and a half ago and now he was suffering the consequences of his actions in a way he never could have imagined. It was useless to deny his attraction to her, yet he could do nothing about it, and maybe that was the price he had to pay for his guilt.

Her voice from the bed called him away from his dark thoughts. "You've done so much for me."

The soft, lilting tone should have warned him that it wasn't as simple as that, but there was something about her vulnerability that drew him, and he heard himself say, "If there's anything else I can do..." his words trailed off awkwardly. What could she possibly want from him other than a place to stay?

"Actually, there is. You can help me with my work while I'm here."

"I don't know much about anthropology."

"Maybe not, but you must know about Seminole folklore."

"Well then, perhaps I could make a contribution to the Everglades Research Center."

"I mean no, I won't take you around."

He knew now what more she could want from him, and it was far worse than he could have imagined. Suddenly she was so much more than merely a beautiful, vulnerable woman who had tumbled into his life. She was dangerous.

If she delved deeply enough, she might uncover the legend about the panther, a tale his people fiercely guarded from outsiders because of its frightening implications. But worse was the possibility that she might discover the truth about him and loathe him for it. He feared that she might see something of him in the legend, as he had come to see himself. That the same proud arrogance that sealed the ancient warrior's fate had doomed him, as well. That the warrior's curse to wander the earth as only part human was no worse than his own fate to live his life only partly alive.

He fought to keep his voice level so that she would not know the turmoil into which her unwitting request had plunged him. "The swamp is no place for someone who can't see."

"That's why I'm asking you to help me."

Damn it. Did she have to sound so unprotected? So in need of his help? "We'll see," he said roughly. "Maybe when you're feeling better." His mind worked rapidly to figure a way out of this mess he was suddenly in. Who knew how long it would

Chapter 5

It was a place that wasn't on the way to anywhere else. You had to go there on purpose, not that anyone ever did.

John used his paddle to press the nose of the canoe against a wall of saw grass, but the stalks were higher than John and Rennie's heads and wouldn't budge. Eventually, his strength prevailed and the walls parted, and little "saws" scratched at their arms as they moved through it.

Rennie knew now why John had insisted she wear his long-sleeved denim shirt. She'd been hesitant at first to accept it, when that wild and earthy scent of his had wafted up from the supple fabric to fill her head with undisciplined thoughts. She was glad to be wearing it, though, for not only did it offer her

watching slowly die. But for now it was still there and teeming with life.

Rennie cocked her head to the side and listened. There was a little plop in the water. "What's that?"

"A yellow-bellied turtle just dived off the rock it was sunning itself on," he answered.

A screech from above drew her attention skyward. "And that?"

"An osprey. Clinging to the edge of an elaborate nest. She doesn't appreciate our company."

She turned her head toward a rustling that came from a crook in the forest.

"Baby alligators," he said, "fighting their way across the water lettuce."

The calm green place that John described offered its heart to Rennie's troubled soul. She couldn't see the towering palms, the live oaks and sweet gums, the moss-draped cypresses or the gumbo limbos that he said were there, but she felt them as keenly as if she could. Out here life didn't seem so terribly complicated at all. She leaned back in the canoe, savoring the sun's warmth on her cheeks and listening to John Panther's deep-throated voice describe the sounds and sights that were all around them.

She didn't know what connection existed between the wild and distant place and the man who guided her through it on this early summer morning, but from the sad and loving way in which he spoke about it, she suspected that his attachment had to do with more than just his people's history.

was something she was trying desperately to do in the aftermath of her eye-opening experience with Craig, not an easy thing to do when she also felt like the world's biggest fool.

"The Seminoles won't surrender. They never have."

"I just meant that what used to be is often an illusion, and the quicker we know it, the better off we are."

"I'm under no illusions myself," he said. "I've seen too much change. When I was a kid, I had this little scruffy brown dog that would lie down in the middle of State Road 7 a good hour before the next car came along. These days, I doubt a dog would make it across the busy street alive, let alone lie down in the middle of it. Today, concrete-block homes have replaced the old cypress chickees, and Seminole women have swapped their beaded necklaces for gold ones."

"You make it sound so dismal."

"First came the white hunters who wiped out huge flocks of wading birds in a matter of hours and slaughtered alligators and panthers and white-tailed deer by the thousands. Then there were the developers, carving canals deep into the swamp, digging for the dirt that would reshape the coastal areas and change the Seminoles' world forever. Then came the missionaries who told us to give up the old ways. So if I make it sound dismal, that's because it is. But don't get me wrong. I love this place. There's

it was the only thing left after he was gone. My knowledge about panthers is just a coincidence.''

Yes, but what a shocking coincidence it was. Who could have guessed when a small boy took his father's name as a means to hold on to him that the name would come to mean so much more? He had to change the subject fast.

"You know, the best way to get the feel of the Everglades is to slog through them, to get down in the muck with mud in your shoes and walls of orchids brushing your shoulders. I have some hip boots back at the cabin. Maybe tomorrow, instead of paddling, we'll walk through the swamp."

"Walk? But aren't there alligators, and snakes, and...things?"

"I know my way around well enough to keep us out of trouble, but if you'd rather not, we don't have to."

"I don't know about walking around hip-deep in the water, but I'd like to see this place," she said. "I mean *really* see it."

"Maybe someday you will."

Rennie sighed. The skin around her eyes was healing nicely, thanks to the tannic acid from the leaves of the sweet gum that John simmered and then smoothed over it each morning, followed by cold clay poultices. She was getting physically stronger every day. But it would take a different kind of strength to return to her former life and con-

like who he was, and what he looked like, and where he went night after night, leaving her alone in the cabin with unanswered questions and empty longings.

Four-winged orange dragonflies danced above the water's surface. The saw grass stretched for mile upon mile, broken in places by scattered clumps of palms and wax-myrtle bushes. As John paddled through the maze of watery paths, he was grateful for Rennie's curiosity and a chance to explain the sounds around them and share with her some of the knowledge he had acquired as a biologist. It helped take his mind off the fact that once again she had gotten to him, and that despite his vow to maintain his distance, here they were, alone together in the swamp. To his dismay he found that the attraction he had confessed to in a weak moment was only heightened when the sunlight tinted her cheeks with a warm pink and poured over her hair in a wash of gold.

In the shaded rooms of the cabin he hadn't realized how much her tawny hair resembled the panther's coat in color. But out here, without the tangle of branches overhead to obscure the sun's rays, he was struck by it, and by the realization that this woman was as dangerous to him as that damned cat.

"There are twelve species of frogs in the Everglades," he said, "six species of lizards, twenty-four species of spiders, and twenty-six species of snakes,

out the cackle of the gallinules that were perched in the tall cypress trees.

The airboat slowed to a halt along the soggy bank, and Billie Gopher climbed down into the shallow water. He was used to inaccessible places that could not be reached by automobile. A lifetime spent trekking through the Everglades had taught him that the fastest and easiest way to get around was on the water. In the old days he used to paddle. These days, he relied on the air propellers to get him where he wanted to go.

Billie Gopher had come into the world beneath a birthing pole sixty-eight years ago, at a time when the medicine men used to take the mixed blood babies into the swamp and leave them there to die. When they came for him, his mother had turned them away with a shotgun.

He came from a line of doctors. His great uncle and grandfather had been doctors. His mother and aunts were medicine ladies. There was never any question of what he would do with his life.

He saw early on that the ancient remedies yielded by the swamp could not cure the white man's diseases that were killing his people, so at the age of thirteen, barely able to read or speak English, with the help of a white uncle, he enrolled in an Indian school hundreds of miles away from home.

Today, fifty-five years later, there was a medical degree from the University of Illinois on the wall at

didn't see the reproachful look he aimed at John, but his voice was mellow and comforting. It was the kind of voice that drew its listener closer, as if it had a secret it wanted to share. "How are you feeling?"

"Tired," she answered.

He came forward until he was standing before her. "That's understandable."

He was a tall man. She knew that from the distance she judged his words to travel. There was a faintly familiar scent about him of the swamp, and she knew that anyone who spent that much time in this place to absorb its essence into his skin could only be Indian.

"Let's see what's what, shall we?"

He took her hands in his and guided her to her feet. His touch was gentle and assured, with none of the tension that was in John's touch. He led her to the bed. She sat down on the edge and he pulled the chair up before her. Gently he peeled the gauze from her eyes and turned her face toward the light from the window.

"I see that someone has been taking good care of you. Your skin is healing very nicely. From the redness and blisters I observed when I first examined you, those were second-degree burns you sustained."

"I waited until the healing started before applying aloe vera," said John.

"That's correct. Aloe on second-degree burns,

the information and realized that she didn't know his name.

"You can call me Dr. Billie. Everyone else does. We don't stand on ceremony here."

That's what John had told her when she had first regained consciousness and had asked his name, except his tone had been considerably less friendly than Dr. Billie's.

"Thank you, Dr. Billie. I appreciate everything you've done for me."

"I'm only doing my job."

"It wasn't always this easy, though, was it?" said John.

Dr. Billie chuckled. "You got that right. There was a time when I would have been shot at just for showing up. Back in the fifties there were only about four hundred Seminoles left. On Mondays I'd mix my medicines and on Tuesdays I'd head out of Miami along the Tamiami Trail to where they lived. The old men used to block my way with rifles, but eventually, they couldn't deny the healing power of the small white pills I made them swallow or the paste I spread on their cuts or the needles I stuck in their arms. Soon they welcomed me into their villages. Some even traveled miles to get their insulin shots or aspirin from me. I owe my thanks to Lorena Osceola for being brave enough to be my first patient. John and his brother used to come to me when they were kids. Of course, I don't see much of John ever since..."

plain the sadness she heard resonating in every word, and maybe somehow justify this crazy attraction she felt for him.

"I'm not hungry," she said sullenly.

He went to the table and looked down at the bowl of half-eaten, cold soup. "When I go out tonight, I'll bring back some meat."

Sarcastically she responded, "Going hunting?"

John's dark hair sliced across his forehead as his head whipped around. "Why do you say that?"

"No offense to whatever meat you might bring back from the swamp, but I'd prefer chicken from the store."

He laughed at his own uptightness. "I wasn't planning on hunting anything in the swamp for you to eat. Actually, I was thinking of stopping at a grocery store on my way back."

"I thought there isn't anything around here for miles."

"There isn't. I have to go over to Big Cypress later to see someone."

"Big Cypress is the reservation, isn't it?"

"Yes."

"Are you going to see Lorena Osceola?"

"Yes."

"Who is she?"

"My mother."

He was hoping that she wouldn't ask to come along. He wasn't ready to take her there with him. There would be too many questions, from both Ren-

as far away from me as you could get. I don't blame you. I must be some sight. A blind mess with stringy hair, wearing clothes you were kind enough to lend me but are way too big, stumbling around like an idiot.''

He wanted to tell her that to him she was the most beautiful thing he'd seen in a long time. That the sight of her wearing one of his shirts made him feel good in spite of himself. That when he came in at daybreak after an unsuccessful night hunting the panther, he would stand there and watch her sleeping, the fan of her hair across his pillow, the rise and fall of her chest, and listen to the little sounds she made in her sleep, and he would wish more than anything to be lying there next to her, with her tawny head nestled in the crook of his arm. But he said nothing, for as quickly as the feeling overwhelmed him, that was as fast as it departed, chased away by the ever-present thought that wishing wouldn't make it so. A woman like her deserved more than a man like him could give. Maggie had found that out the hard way.

''It has nothing to do with you,'' he said. ''I told you, I work at night.''

She gave a little sigh of resignation. ''That's all right. I understand.''

''Feeling sorry for yourself?''

It wasn't easy owning up to the mistakes she had made. The hard part was admitting to herself just how wrong she'd been. And if she felt just a little

Chapter 6

Rennie awoke with a start, heart thumping, feeling disoriented.

Where was she? What time was it? What was that aroma in the air? It wasn't anything like the perfume that permeated her Palm Beach condo. And then she remembered. She wasn't in her Palm Beach condo. She was out in the middle of nowhere, and it was the smell of that vast nowhere, the sweet, musky scent of earth and water, that invaded her senses.

The tension ebbed from her muscles. She was miles and miles, and light years, it seemed, away from that place that was filled with bad memories and cutting disappointments, the biggest disappointment of all being the one she felt with herself over all those wrong choices.

man whose face she couldn't even see, and sobering to realize that the attraction came not from what he looked like, but from how he made her feel—safe, protected, yet a little reckless.

She could tell by the feel of the cool, damp air against her skin that it was night, and by the acute silence that she was alone, as she was every other night when she awoke to find him gone.

The truth was that whenever he was gone, she missed his deep, remorseful voice and the hesitant, almost shy, way in which he took her hand in his to guide her about. She missed his stories of the swamp, the gentleness with which he changed the dressing over her eyes, the scent of earth and wind that came from his hair, the sound of his footsteps across the cypress planks. She missed the air of mystery about him that spawned a host of questions, like where did he really go every night, why was he so reluctant to talk about himself, and what did he look like? In short, she missed *him,* a thought that was as arousing as it was worrisome.

She turned her head on the pillow and drifted off again, only to be awakened a short time later by a sound outside. She lay very still, straining to hear, as goose bumps raced across her flesh. When the sound did not come again, she relaxed. It was probably just a raccoon or an opossum scurrying about in the dark.

She remembered the time she found a baby raccoon in the backyard at their summer home. Her

It hadn't taken Craig's investigator that long to find her.

Sick with fear, she didn't know what to do. She knew the kind of men who worked for Craig, men like himself, ruthless and unsympathetic. In her sightless state it would have been very easy for him to force her to go with him. And once back in Craig's control, unable to see, she'd be powerless to flee. She had to do something. She couldn't just stand there, barefoot and wearing nothing but one of John's T-shirts, for him to walk in and take her.

It took every ounce of strength she had for her to remain there, listening and waiting. She heard the footsteps move off to the side of the cabin, and then around back. Now! Do it now!

Her hand shook as it grasped the doorknob. She felt a soft rush of summer air when she opened the door. Without thinking, guided only by sheer terror, she ran from the cabin.

The ground beneath her bare feet was moist and pliant from a rain shower earlier in the evening. The air she sucked into her lungs was humid and warm. With her arms outstretched, fingers splayed before her, she ran blindly. She stepped on a stone and bit back the pain that ripped through the sole of her foot. With a thud she ran smack into the trunk of a tree and fell to the ground, panting with fear. Stumbling to her feet, she whirled in all directions, not knowing where she was or which way to go.

A strangled sob escaped her throat, but it was

wrist in his strong grip and attempted to pry her hands loose from around his neck, but when it became clear that she would not...could not...let go, he stopped trying.

He sank down onto the bed beside her and let her hold fast to him, wrapping his own arms around her, using his quiet strength to quell her fears and quiet her sobbing. Until she was perfectly still in his arms, almost as if she were asleep. And even if he had wanted to let go, he couldn't. She wasn't sleeping, only exhausted. The minutes passed and she gradually came back to herself until she was able to speak. Her voice scratched at the back of her throat and emerged a hoarse whisper.

"I was so afraid. So afraid. I didn't know what was out there."

He felt her tremble and tightened his hold reassuringly. "I told you, there's nothing to be afraid of out there. Didn't we go over all the sounds?"

"Yes, but it was human."

"It was me."

"I didn't know. You weren't here, and I thought it was—" She bit back the rest of her words. "What time is it?"

"I don't know. A little past midnight. Why?"

"You usually don't return until dawn. What are you doing back so early?"

She felt the subtle tensing of his muscles and sensed the evasion in his voice when he said, "The animal I was—" he caught himself about to say

The questions, asked in that fragile, beautiful voice, were becoming too painful for him, and he was torn by an impulse to tell her about his irrational need to wander the swamp night after night in search of the panther that killed his wife, and suffer the consequences. She had a right to be curious. But he also had the right to keep his private hell to himself.

His resolve was sorely tested, however, when her trembling body was leaning exquisitely against his and he could hear the breathless vulnerability in her voice. He struggled to keep his emotions at bay. Without realizing the consequences, he asked, "Any other questions?"

She tilted her head up at him, and through the moonlight that came in through the window her face looked pale and beautiful. "I want to know what you look like," she said shyly.

"There's not much to tell. Dark hair. Dark eyes."

"No, I mean—" She hesitated, embarrassed to say what she really meant. She moved out of his arms. Her grasp unlocked from around his neck and her hands slid slowly across his shoulders, coming to rest on either side of his face. "May I?"

He knew what she wanted and groaned inwardly. But he understood its importance. With a brief nod, he said, "Go ahead."

She placed her hands tentatively at his jaw and moved them slowly up the sides of his face, the tips of her fingers brushing hair that was thick and fine, like silken rope. She swept one loose lock aside to

He emitted a long, low breath he'd been holding trapped in his lungs. "The Seminoles believe that a person is responsible for his or her own fate, and that it's what you do with your life that determines your fate."

If that were true, she thought, then was it possible that all her mistakes had been for the dual purpose of teaching her about herself, and leading her here...to him? If it was her fate to be here with him, then maybe it was also meant to be that she give in to this crazy attraction she had for him. For the first time in her life she realized that maybe she was responsible for her own fate after all.

Perhaps it was precisely because she couldn't see that she felt suddenly bolder. It was kind of like the feeling she got wearing sunglasses—knowing that nobody could see her eyes made her feel absurdly safe and somehow braver than usual. She wet her lips and tilted her face up at him.

"And what do the Seminoles say about two people coming together for only one night? Would they say it was expediency or fate?"

His whole body tensed. "They would say that a man and woman coming together can change the course of the world and must not be taken lightly."

"I don't want to change the whole world. Only my world."

There was a soft plea in her voice that touched something deep inside of him. What he told her about people being responsible for their own fate

any more words or explanations. It was as if this moment had been decreed from the start, as if every minute had been leading up to the feel of her lips beneath his as he brought his mouth down upon hers.

She met his kiss greedily, lips parting and tongue searching, teasing, tasting. His flavor was as sweet as she had imagined. She felt the erratic pounding of his heart against her own, and it filled her with a feeling of desire and power that she had never experienced before. She made no protest when he laid her back against the mattress and covered her body with the lean length of his.

She had wanted to connect with another human being, to feel needed and wanted and necessary, with no questions asked and no regrets. But this was rapidly turning into so much more.

She strained against him. There was a sudden urgency in her, a dire necessity that went beyond logic or reason. Passion was too mild a word for what she felt. Excitement barely described it. Even when his kiss grew stronger, lips almost brutally devouring hers, she returned his demand with her own. There was nothing but him—his lips, his arms, his scent, the hard bite of his arousal against her. In a detached part of her mind came a fleeting thought that it wasn't just the connection she wanted, it was him.

The strength she felt in his lean, hard muscles warned her that he would not be an easy lover. But she didn't want easy. She'd had that all her life.

working in incredible unison until she was writhing beneath him.

She had never felt this kind of need before. To have his hands on her body and his mouth on her mouth were, at this moment, the most important things in the world to her, save one.

Dragging her mouth from his, she placed her hands at his shoulders and pushed him back, feeling his resistance and pushing him harder.

Immediately awash with confusion and guilt and shame for having misread her signals, he staggered up onto his elbows and looked down at her, cursing the bandages that concealed her eyes, which otherwise might have given him a clue as to what was coming. "I'm sorry," he said raggedly. "I thought...I didn't mean to..."

She interrupted in a breathless whisper, "No, don't be. It's not that. I want to see the rest of you."

It took a moment for the impact of her statement to hit him. When it did, he was relieved to know he'd been wrong about her intentions, and near out of his mind with arousal. He rolled off her, quickly undressed and sank back onto the bed beside her, his chest rising and falling heavily from his rough breathing.

Again he was forced to remain rigid while her hands did a slow exploration, not hesitantly and shyly the way she had touched his face, but with a boldness he hadn't known she possessed. He assumed that her fragile, confused state was to blame

Without gentleness or calmness, they sought each other, lips taking, kisses possessive, hungers urgent. The molten pleasure that ruled her became like white liquid heat surging through her, searing her from the inside out. With a strength she didn't know she possessed, she rolled on top of him, then he on her, until they were tangled in each other's arms and legs and passion. She heard her name tear from his lips and words she didn't understand, Seminole words, muffled against her. At the moment of his possession she cried out in a voice, that to her dazed and drunken mind, didn't even sound like her own. Higher and faster they climbed, his mouth clinging to hers, swallowing her moans and fusing them with his own, both consumed with the shock and power of it.

Even after he rolled off her, she couldn't stop the shudders. They continued to speed through her long after he lay silent and still beside her. What had happened between them had never happened to her before. In some intuitive place within herself she knew it never would again with any other man. It was his strength and his untamed lovemaking and his complexity that made him so unique, and gave her a glimpse into a part of herself she had not known existed.

Her voice split the stillness. "What are you thinking?"

He stirred beside her. "To tell the truth, I was trying not to think."

Chapter 7

"**Y**ou want me to *what?*"

John tried to keep the panic from rising in his voice. After what happened between them last night, and the reproaches he heaped upon himself the following morning, the last thing he needed was this.

Rennie had been reticent much of the morning, showing none of the unrestraint she had exhibited the night before, remembering and regretting. She pushed around the flakes of cereal in her bowl with the tip of the spoon, her face averted shyly, and repeated, "I want you to teach me the folklore of your people."

John stood rigid by the window, staring at the sunlight that slanted through the branches, not really seeing it. He knew what was happening to him. No,

cause, well, frankly, it intrigues me. There was an old Seminole man who worked for the university as a night janitor. He's the one who got me interested a few years back. Sometimes, when I'd be working late, he would come in to clean up and we'd talk for a while. His stories were fascinating, but there was something he wasn't telling me.''

John turned back to her. She was too slender, he thought, too vulnerable despite last night's show of passion and strength, to deal with the threat of what could happen.

"I can't imagine what that might be," he said.

She thought she detected evasion in his voice, but after last night she wasn't sure of anything. "Well then, do you know of anyone I can ask who would know?''

John shook his head, silently repeating his vow to see her through this and keep her safe until it was time for her to leave. And then he'd get out of her life. Until then, he had to maneuver carefully around her. The thought of telling her the stories himself was bad enough considering his own tragic and lurid tale, but having someone else tell her could be worse.

His people kept the legend of the panther to themselves, learning as children to guard it from the outside world, for it was a sacred lesson that carried a grim reality. But what if someone made an unwitting slip of the tongue? What if one thing said here and another said there led Rennie to put the clues to-

roosters crowed and went to bed when the sun set. Today she lived in a modest, yet comfortable, house on the Big Cypress Reservation. The cypress trees were gone, but she had all the amenities of modern life.

She answered the knock on her door, not knowing what to expect. Her son had sounded anxious on the phone, speaking the mixture of Miccosukee and Creek that was their native tongue, telling her that he was coming by that afternoon and he'd be bringing someone with him. When pressed, he admitted that, yes, it had to do with the white woman who was staying at the cabin. The one he had called Billie Gopher in to see, the one he tried to avoid in conversation.

Lorena knew the terrible shame her son carried over what he perceived to be his hand in his wife's death. In these past few months, however, he'd begun to come by more frequently, and she thought that maybe he was finding a way out of his lonely exile. But whenever he spoke in steely tones of his need for revenge, she realized how far he still had to go, and it gave her cause to worry. Why had he brought the white woman to see her, and what was it about the woman that had him so uneasy?

He knocked out of respect as he always did, even though he was welcome without invitation and her door was never locked. She opened the door and saw his unsmiling face, and knew immediately that something was wrong.

spoke, hands that had not known a day of hard labor in her life. She was dressed in jeans that fit her too perfectly to have been someone else's, and then Lorena remembered something John had said a few days ago about stopping off at the Army Navy store in Fort Lauderdale. Interesting that he would know her size so well. She wore a white T-shirt with a denim shirt she recognized as John's over it.

Lorena learned early in life not to trust outsiders, but she had also learned not to judge in haste, so with the flat inflection and measured tone of many English-speaking Seminoles, she said, "The glasses are a good idea. I used to be a nurse, but I'm also a woman."

Rennie was glad that the woman understood why it had been important for her not to be all bandaged up and looking like the poor blind woman today. Lorena was, after all, John's mother. She'd never met Craig's mother. Divorced from Craig's father, the woman lived on the Côte d'Azur with her young French lover and was the scandal of Palm Beach society. Being taken by a man to meet his mother was a brand-new experience, and Rennie was unusually conscious of herself.

A moment of silence passed in which Rennie sat helplessly in darkness and John and Lorena exchanged a worried look.

"I'll bet you two are hungry," said Lorena. "John, why don't you and Rennie have a seat at the table and I'll go get the food."

"It looks like you've made enough for an army again," John teased.

Lorena chuckled. "To this day I have trouble preparing it in small quantities because when I learned to make it from the village women, they used ten pounds of flour for one batch of dough. We had a big family to feed. With the grandparents and parents and siblings there was close to thirty of us."

As she spoke, Lorena watched John place his hands over Rennie's and guide them to platters of food, as easily and naturally as if he had done it a hundred times before. Her heart filled with pride at his caring nature. Her son was a good, honest man who had done one wrong thing in his life and was paying heavily for it.

It was good that he had found someone whose need was more imperative than his own, that he was able to see past his grief and sorrow to look after the white woman. But one look at his face and Lorena's heart sank. His feelings shone in the barest uplifting of his full lips in a smile he wasn't even aware of. They were written in the dark eyes that lingered overly long on the white woman's face, before disappearing self-consciously beneath a fan of thick lashes. Lorena didn't want her son to hurt anymore. A year and a half was enough. But was this the answer? She had hoped he would eventually find a woman to make him forget his vow of vengeance, not one like this who would only make him remember.

a curious nature and knew how to get to her without consciously doing it.

"You don't have to eat that," Lorena suggested when she saw Rennie lift a piece of fry bread to her mouth. "It's fried in lard and you're probably not used to it."

"John has it at the cabin all the time," said Rennie. "Now I know where he gets it. I'll admit it took a little getting used to, but no more so than the mushy spaghetti I make." She gave a little self-deprecating laugh. "We've both made some adjustments to our diets."

Lorena noticed the unconscious familiarity in Rennie's voice as she spoke about herself and John. It was almost as if they were a twosome and neither of them knew it.

"I think it's wonderful that you keep to the old way of cooking," said Rennie. "There's precious little of old ways of anything in my family, such as it is."

"No customs?" Lorena questioned. "No holiday rituals?"

"When my mother was alive, the holiday rituals were grand, ostentatious, impersonal displays of material goodness that included about two hundred of her closest friends. Not the kind of thing a kid looks forward to every year, if you know what I mean. That's why I'm so fascinated by Seminole culture and its emphasis on the family."

Lorena nodded knowingly. "I remember the les-

and Lorena would have been able to read her thoughts in them.

"Ah-Tha-Thi-Ki," Lorena said, snapping the moment of silence that threatened to stretch too long. "That's what the museum is called. But there's not much there, anyway. The Seminoles are unique in what they haven't kept. Our traditions are passed down from mother to child by word of mouth. Our art is represented in personal possessions, clothing primarily, and cooking utensils. But those material items are always buried with the dead. Collecting another's possession is disrespectful and unlucky."

"There doesn't seem to be much documented history, either," said Rennie.

Lorena nodded solemnly. "We have lost priceless knowledge of our people because in the past we failed to properly record our history so that we can always remember."

"I would love to hear what *you* remember."

Lorena sneaked a look at John, but his eyes were downcast and unreadable. "You have a healthy curiosity."

John's gaze lifted. "Rennie is an anthropologist." He took a sip of *sofkee,* a drink made with wild oranges, licking the sweetness from his lips the way he'd been doing since he was a boy. "She's studying the culture of our people. The myths and legends, to be exact. I thought maybe you could, you know, share with her some of the...stories."

Now she knew the cause of the apprehension

Lorena's dark eyes flashed a warning, but her voice was soft, gentle, understanding. "Be careful."

"I told her I'd help her."

"Go keep your pretty friend company," his mother told him, "while I go inside to get something."

He'd only been gone a few minutes, but more and more his absences felt interminable to Rennie. Sitting alone at the table in a house filled with strange smells and customs made her realize all over again how little she knew about him. When he returned, she asked, "Do you see much of your brother?"

"Tommy's cattle keep him busy."

"What about cousins or uncles?"

"I have a great-uncle who grows citrus in Palm Beach County, an uncle who's a computer programmer in Chicago, and cousins scattered all over the place. My people are adaptable and pragmatic. They're as at home raising cattle, growing crops and living in cities as they are canoeing through the Everglades."

"Our entire way of life is tied to the Everglades." Lorena entered the room and placed on the table something wrapped in fading tissue paper. "My people have lived in the heart of the Everglades for generations. Some call the Everglades a swamp. We call it our mother."

With a reverent touch she opened the fragile folds of paper to reveal a dress inside. "This is made in the traditional patchwork way." Reaching across the

brought back so many remembrances of good times and bad. She could see five-year-old Tom grasping on to the skirt, the fabric bunched in his small fist, two-year-old John standing off by himself, solitary and somber even at that young age. She had taught her boys to deal with the white world, but to live in the Indian world, and to know that there was good and bad in everything. They had grown into self-sufficient, strong men. But while her older son knew about the age-old battle of good and evil from the stories he'd been told, her younger son knew first-hand just how terrible it could be. It brought to mind the legend of the sun and the moon and of the young Miccosukee woman who, like John, learned about good and evil the hard way. Lorena drew in her breath and began to speak.

"There was, and is, and will be the Spirit Being. He is one yet many. He is visible and invisible. He is the physical and the immaterial. He is the good in the world...and the evil. There was a Miccosukee woman who was possessed of great charm and beauty, but she was more devoted to this than she was to the welfare of her sons. Upon seeing her, the sun was so struck by her incredible beauty that he forgot his wife, the moon, and invited the Micco-sukee woman to sit beside him in the sky. The Mic-cosukee woman, being vain and ambitious, accepted. But when the Spirit Being learned that the sun had forsaken his wife and the mortal woman had dared to usurp the place of a goddess, he sentenced

ceptible quiver of her lip. But Lorena was looking directly at her son as she spoke.

Rennie cleared her throat and said, "There seems to be a universal theme of good and evil running through the Seminole legends I've heard. What can you tell me about a legend centering around a panther?"

Lorena stared dumbfounded, not knowing what to say.

John's face paled, and he sat there in stunned silence when he realized, at the same time as his mother did, that Rennie already knew of the existence of the panther legend.

"Remember that old Seminole man I told you about?" Rennie said to John. "The night janitor?" she prompted, when the only response she received from him was silence. "Just this morning, I told you—"

"I remember." His voice was strained and tense.

"Well, he mentioned it once when he'd had too much to drink. When I questioned him about it the next time I saw him, he clammed up, saying only that accordingly to the legend, deep in the swamp lives something that cannot be imagined. That must be quite a story." .

The legs of the chair scraped the tile floor as Lorena got up and began to hastily wrap the dress. As she swept the bundle into her arms, she paused to look at her son, her heart aching to see the look of stunned pain that was on his face. Quietly she said,

Chapter 8

"I just don't understand it."

Rennie had to speak loudly to be heard over the hum of the airboat as she and John buzzed across the alligator-laden waters, skimming over vegetation.

John guided the boat along the smooth water through a thick cypress forest that was alive with birds. He tried to lose himself in the glowing, almost green sunlight that filtered through the trees, and to forget, for the moment, the promise he'd made to help Rennie with her work.

How could he have agreed to such a stupid thing? What was it about her that had him doing things he swore he'd never do? That she brought out his protective instincts was obvious, painfully so, when he

And as he had discovered one fateful night, an eager lover.

But the same curiosity that gave him such a thrill was also a source of constant worry to him, for by keeping his promise to guide her to remote places in her quest for myths and legends, he was breaking the vow he'd made to himself to remain detached and unaffected.

"I don't understand," Rennie repeated. "You told me your mother knows all the legends, yet when I questioned her about the panther legend, she acted as if she didn't know what I was talking about."

He'd taken her to see his mother because he knew that while she could tell Rennie some fascinating stories, she would not share with an outsider the legend that carried such an awful truth. "Maybe she doesn't know such a legend," he offered, feeling more and more guilty for the lies and evasions.

"I may be blind," Rennie complained, "but I'm not stupid. I'm telling you, there was something she wasn't saying. Why is everyone so closemouthed?"

His emotions were guarded, but he answered truthfully. "You're an outsider. You're white. My people had three wars in forty years with your people. Those wars destroyed our families and separated my people. We've come to accept much of what we find in outside society and use it in our own way, but the elders, the ones who remember the old ways and what it was like to live without that outside

was distressing to think she'd been wrong in reading him, until she thought about Craig and remembered how easy it was to see only what she wanted to see.

Dusk was settling over the Everglades when they arrived back at the cabin. John guided the airboat to the edge of the shore and killed the engine. A static silence greeted them as he slid down into the shallow water. Without a word, he reached up for her, hands encircling her waist to lift her down from the boat. The green water lilies parted as he carried her to the shore.

Overhead a sudden flapping of wings drew Rennie's attention skyward. Grateful for something to divert her mind from the strong arms that held her, she proclaimed, "A great egret."

"Very good," he said.

She strained to identify the rustling she heard nearby. "A marsh rabbit?"

It would take a familiarity with the swamp that could only be achieved in a lifetime to recognize that sound, but he admired her for trying. "Fiddler crabs," he said, "scuttling over the paw prints of the raccoons that tried to catch them last night."

He let her down beside him. The ground was unexpectedly soft and pliant, and she stumbled. His arms were back around her in a flash, holding her against him while she struggled for balance. Since the other night he had avoided touching her. There was no sense, he reasoned, in conjuring up all those emotions caused by the mere feel of her. But with

feel of the air, and what Rennie felt now told her it would soon be dark, and she would soon be alone.

"I'll start dinner," she said. "Spaghetti?"

John laughed in spite of himself. "I'll make a deal with you. I'll cook and you can set the table."

The rare and beautiful sound of his unguarded laughter took the edge off the tension that was palpable in the air. "Are you trying to tell me something?"

"Only that you make lousy spaghetti."

"My expertise lies in more complicated, extravagant dishes," she boasted. "You've never tasted my beef Wellington or my Grand Marnier soufflé. When you do, you'll forget spaghetti ever existed."

"I've never tasted anybody's Grand Marnier soufflé," he admitted.

"And it's no wonder, cooped up in this place. I know, I know, you have your work to do out here."

His work wasn't the only reason he had chosen this sanctuary, but he didn't tell her that. "If you've screamed down the water slide at one of those theme parks, or bungie-jumped off a cliff, I guess a million and a half acres of soggy plants might seem tame by comparison. But 'cooped up' isn't exactly the way I'd describe it. I've found myself watching the Everglades sky with as much excitement as I've watched for alligators. There's so much of it that the vista seems almost top heavy, like it might tip over. In any other forest it takes a bird two, maybe three seconds, to fly from one tree to another and be lost

demons, he was entitled to his, and it irked him when she changed the subject, unwittingly turning the tables on him.

"You don't remember hearing anything about a panther legend when you were growing up?" she asked as she felt her way around the table, setting it for two with napkins and utensils.

Her question made his dilemma over whether to go out or to stay even more difficult. He knew how dangerous it was to stay there with her and suffer through her questioning, yet the way her cheeks were flushed with exasperation made her even more appealing and harder to resist. She moved about the room like a great cat, angry and graceful in the small space she was by now completely familiar with, his dark eyes following her relentlessly.

"Is it really that important?" he asked.

She took two plates down from the shelf, saying, "Yes. It is. I worked hard for that grant. I'd hate to think it was for nothing."

For the hundredth time he asked himself whether his own pursuit would, in the end, all be for nothing, and if the thirst for vengeance that drove him would ultimately lead to his own undoing. He knew that Rennie's need to know about the legend went beyond her work. It went to the heart of her. To that place inside that said don't ever give up no matter how dismal things seem. He understood because he had such a place inside of him.

He shifted his gaze toward the window. The light

The Silhouette Reader Service™ — Here's how it works:

NO POSTAGE
NECESSARY
IF MAILED
IN THE
UNITED STATES

If offer card is missing write to: Silhouette Reader Service, 3010 Walden Ave., P.O. Box 1867, Buffalo NY 14240-1867

BUSINESS REPLY MAIL

FIRST-CLASS MAIL   PERMIT NO. 717-003   BUFFALO, NY

POSTAGE WILL BE PAID BY ADDRESSEE

SILHOUETTE READER SERVICE

3010 WALDEN AVE

PO BOX 1867

BUFFALO NY 14240-9952

around her waist he pulled her so close that her body seemed molded to his, the fingers of his other hand splayed in her hair, pulling her head back so that his kiss could go still deeper.

She offered no resistance when his lips moved to her throat. The moist heat of his tongue sent swells of pleasure through her as he bent her back from the waist, supporting her in one strong arm while tearing at the buttons of her shirt, sending one arcing into the air in his desperate desire to bare her flesh.

Under his hand her breasts rose and fell with her quickening breath. Taut nipples strained against the heat of his palms. When she thought she could bear no more of the maddening caresses, his mouth came back to hers and she felt herself swept up into his arms, his lips never leaving hers.

He carried her effortlessly to the closest thing, the table. With one sweep of his arm he sent the silverware clattering to the floor. She felt the cool, hard surface of the table at her back, contrasting with the hot, pliant body that covered hers.

Her trembles excited him, but he wanted more. He wanted her hands on him like the last time. He wanted to feel the incredible heat of her, to drown in it, to let it consume him in torrid flames until he forgot everything else except her. He moaned roughly against her flesh when he felt her hand slip between their bodies to grasp him and stoke those flames into an inferno.

She had never felt anything like the surging

ripped open the zipper. When he was as naked as she was, he moved into the space between her legs.

Her responsiveness overwhelmed him. All restraint had fled. All the barriers were broken. With her hand she guided him to the place she needed him to be and arched her hips to deepen his penetration. She heard herself calling his name in a voice that was rough with need. She clung to him mindlessly, a breath away from tears as they soared through space and time.

Later, he carried her to the bed and they lay spent in each other's arms, covered in darkness. There were no lights on in the cabin, and the moon must have been sequestered behind a cloud. As he lay there with his arms wrapped around her, he realized that in the darkness he was as blind as she was. It didn't matter how beautiful she was, only that she was. In all of his memory he had never known a more perfect moment as this one. That very first day when he had carried her bruised and blistered body into the cabin, little could he have known the depth of her passion or the effect it would have on him.

Rennie's breathing slowly leveled as passion turned to contentment. She had often wondered what it was that was missing from her life. Now she knew. This was it, the missing link. He made her feel like a woman, not a woman to manipulate and possess, but a woman who knew how to receive and to give in return. A woman who knew what she

her lips and swallowed, grateful not only for the darkness, but for her blindness, which prevented her from seeing his face as she began to speak.

"I had planned on coming to the Everglades to do research as part of the grant, I just hadn't planned on coming so soon. If I'd been thinking clearly, I never would have taken off in the storm, but when you're desperate and afraid, you do things you never thought you'd do."

"A common affliction," he muttered.

"Yes, but how do you explain the mistakes you make when you're not desperate and afraid, when you think you're happy and realize when it's almost too late that you're not?"

"We all make mistakes, Rennie," he said tautly, thinking of his own fatal error that had led him to this place in his life. "All we can do is learn from them, and if not, then try to live with them as best we can. Besides, you still haven't told me what this big mistake was. Maybe it's not so bad." Whatever her failures were, he knew with cold certainty that they could not be as bad as his own.

"His name is Craig Wolfson." There, it was out. There was no turning back now. "He was my fiancé. We were going to be married in June."

Married. The word ricocheted off his mind like a bullet fired at close range, hitting him harder than he expected. Stop it, he ordered himself. Stop feeling wounded. Very deliberately he shifted his weight slightly away from her. "Were?"

I ignored all the signs of possession, the manipulative nature of the man, the lack of emotion inside of myself, because I thought that marrying Craig was what I was supposed to do. Don't you see, all my life I've been told what I'm supposed to do.''

In the darkness he could see the pale cloud of hair that fanned over his arm and the angle of her cheekbone in the moonlight. A man would be a fool to try to possess her. She was like a delicate butterfly caught in one's hands. If you held tight, you would kill it. But if you opened your hands and showed it the freedom that was there for the taking, it would stay, fluttering its wings in your palm and taking your breath away with its flawless beauty.

"And who told you that you're supposed to be lying here with me?''

"Nobody. It just…happened.''

"Getting hit by a truck just happens,'' he said dryly.

"What are you saying?''

"I'm saying that you're here with me like this right now because you're doing what *you* want to do. You made the decision. Nobody else.''

Rennie considered for a moment what he said, then nodded. "That's true.''

"Why did you do it? To teach him a lesson?''

She jolted away from him and sat up. "Are you suggesting I made love with you to get back at Craig? I never wanted this to happen. I didn't start it.''

around her shoulders. Together they walked back to the bed. Lying down beside her, he pulled her into his embrace and held her.

"That night you ran from the cabin, was it that guy you were afraid of?"

Rennie shivered against him. "You don't know him. He's manipulative and controlling and rich. And he gets what he wants."

"And what he wants is you." It was a statement, not a question, and even as he said it he felt a stab of jealousy. "Don't worry. He can't hurt you."

He wanted to tell her that he would protect her from the man she feared, but what gave him the right, when the mere act of holding her in his arms put her in a danger she couldn't even imagine? Touched by her honesty, there raged within him a battle over whether to share his secret with her. She had a right to know, didn't she, that in her search for a legend, they were both searching for the same thing...the panther.

"You've been so good to me," she said softly. "All the things you've bought for me, I want you to know, I'll pay you back."

Something inside of him rose with anticipation. "And how do you propose to do that?" he said with a gentle laugh.

"When my eyesight returns...or even if it doesn't...I'll have to go back and face my mistakes. And when I do, I'll pay you back every penny."

It wasn't what he expected. The prospect of her

Chapter 9

The morning broke quiet and calm.

John sat with his back pressed against the trunk of a giant cypress tree, oblivious to the cobweb of moss that hung from an overhead branch, and brushed his face in the breeze as he watched the soft buttery light crest the trees and infiltrate the swamp. He hadn't slept a wink all night, but neither had he gone in pursuit of that devil beast. Instead, he just sat there hour after lonely hour, reliving last night over and over again in his mind.

He'd left the cabin in the dead of night after he swore to himself that he wouldn't. He had wanted to stay there with her, God how he'd wanted to. But the sound of her breathing as she slept, the smell of her, the very thought of her was too much to bear,

have been used to them, but he wasn't. Just like he would never get used to the loneliness.

He thought he had it all under control. He told himself that if it ever got too lonely, he could always go to the reservation anytime he wanted to see his mother. And old Willie Cypress came by to visit him every now and then, which helped break up the monotony of his self-imposed exile. But it wasn't until Rennie fell into his life that he realized how all-pervasive that loneliness really was. How it invaded every corner of the cabin, every inch of the swamp, every fiber of his being.

The familiar *shhh* of the saw grass called John away from his dismal thoughts. He drew a breath of warm, humid air deep into his lungs and let it out slowly as his gaze swept the horizon. The Everglades were mysterious to anyone who did not understand their fundamental nature. But to him, born and raised in the vast wetland, there was no mystery here, only life at its purest and most complicated. Even the inexplicability of the panther's vengeance was something he did not question. It simply was.

It was at times like this, when he felt an acute longing deep in his soul, that he saw his beloved Everglades as they really were, a place that was slowly dying, as he was inside. Too little or too much water reached the marsh at the wrong times because of a latticework system of canals that delivered water to homes and front yards and farms, with the Everglades always at the end of the line. When

and canoeing through the pinelands or the mangroves or the slough, each with its own unique atmosphere.

The hammocks were green, fragrant, shady places where he sometimes tugged the canoe ashore and they would sit for a while, she listening to the sounds of nature, he explaining them. She recalled one morning in particular when they had stopped in just such a place. She had lain back on the grass, her arms under her head, thinking wistfully aloud how she could stay there forever, until John told her about the eastern diamondbacks and the black bears that lurked about, and she let out a little yelp of fright, causing his laughter to reverberate through the stillness and her cheeks to redden. But the lighthearted moment was gone as soon as she had asked him about the presence of panthers. In cold, irrefutable silence he had pulled her up by the hand and shoved the canoe back into the water. They had paddled for home without speaking, leaving her to wonder what she had said or done to bring about such an abrupt change in him.

Sometimes she questioned if she would ever understand him. Last night, for instance, he had fairly begged her to make him stay, and even after she did, he left. How could a man who was so unselfish and open in his lovemaking be so closed off to her emotionally? She had thought that by revealing her own private torment, it might clear the way for him to be forthcoming about whatever it was that was

"Who's there?" she said as she slipped them onto her face.

"Just me, miss."

She recognized the voice of Willie Cypress, the old frog hunter who had found her after the plane crash and brought her to John. Willie sometimes stopped by during the day when John was there. He was a cheerful man, if not a little too talkative for her liking. She usually went outside to sit by herself while the two of them conversed in their own language. She didn't feel offended by it. After all, she was the outsider.

"John's not here this morning, Willie," she told him. "Can I offer you something to drink? It feels like it's going to be a hot one today."

"You got a beer?"

John wasn't much of a drinker, but Rennie knew he kept beer in the cabin for Willie's sporadic visits. "Sure. Have a seat."

She found her way easily to the kitchen where she pulled a cold bottle of beer out of the refrigerator. The bottle opener was in the drawer where she knew it would be. Fitting it over the bottle top, she popped the cap off, grateful for John's neatness that had everything in place and made small tasks such as this so much easier.

"It smells like you've been fishing," she said, when she handed Willie the bottle.

He took a swallow, then ran the back of his hand

"Let me tell you, miss, there's freedom and then there's freedom. Me, I've got the freedom to run away from my naggin' wife anytime I want, but I can always go back home. *That's* true freedom."

"But I've met John's mother," Rennie softly protested. "She would let him go back home if he wanted to."

"Lorena? Hell, she's got a heart as big as the Glades. Nah, I wasn't talking about John. Tell me, miss, did you ever believe in something you couldn't see...before you couldn't really see, that is?"

She believed in John Panther, and with his help she was beginning to believe in her own instincts. Choosing her words carefully, she said, "I believe it's not always necessary to experience that which you know in your heart to be true."

"Well, there you have it."

Rennie shook her head in confusion. "What does that have to do with freedom?"

"Like I said, there's different kinds of freedom. John, he comes and goes as he pleases for reasons of his own. That damned cat, now, he comes and goes, too. At night he comes on all fours. You'd think that was the greatest freedom of all, an animal doin' what an animal does. But when daybreak comes..." He snapped his fingers in the air. "Poof. Gone. Freedom? I don't think so."

"What cat? What are you talking about?"

Willie dropped his voice to a low, confiding tone.

"Hell, no, I ain't seen nothin'. I'm just sayin' it's one of them legends that you either believe or you don't believe. Me, I'm inclined to believe it. But maybe I've been in the Glades too long, huh?"

Suddenly everything was forgotten, the smell of fish he brought in with him, the rain that had begun to fall, the frantic beating of her heart. "Can I get you another beer?"

"Don't mind if I do."

This time her hands shook as she pried the cap off the bottle. The grant depended on this. She needed something to take back with her, something to show her colleagues that all her work had not been in vain, something to show her doubting step-father how serious she was about her profession, something to prove to herself that anything was possible.

She returned with another cold beer and said as calmly as she could, "So, tell me about the panther legend."

"The Seminoles place great store in their legends," he told her. "But this one scares them. Maybe it's 'cause they know they could wind up like that poor warrior if they ain't careful." He took several long swallows of beer, which helped loosen his tongue even further.

"There was this warrior, see. And he killed this panther. But he was so proud and stupid that he didn't say a prayer to the Spirit Being. Now, the Indians, they got this thing about sayin' a prayer

stincts about him before, she doubted them no longer. But the Seminoles believing in the legend was one thing. Believing it herself was something else. She tilted her head at him and said challengingly, ''All right, tell me this. If the Seminoles believe such a creature exists, do they know where it is?''

''Nobody knows,'' said Willie. ''Out there in the swamp someplace.''

''If he walks as a man by day, does anyone ever see him?''

''Who knows? Maybe yes. Maybe no. He could be anyone. Your next-door neighbor. Your husband. The person you trust the most. Most likely he's a loner. Someone whose absence at night arouses no suspicion.''

''It's intriguing, I'll grant you that,'' she said. ''But a man who turns into a cat?'' She shook her head skeptically. ''I don't know.''

''Well, you believe what you want,'' he said. ''But I'm tellin' you, some things just can't be explained. If you ever meet someone who's just a little bit puzzlin', a man with somethin' to hide, ask yourself, could it be him?''

Rennie laughed at the mystery in his tone. ''How do I know it's not you?''

''Me? I ain't no cat. Besides, I don't go out every night. Some nights, when I'm looking for a little lovin', if you know what I mean, I stay home and

good, miss. That John, he's a little strange sometimes, but he's a good healer.'' She heard the door
close behind him.

For several minutes she stood rooted to her spot,
not knowing what to do. If she told John what Willie
had told her, it might only drive a wedge further
between them. If John possessed such a deep and
deadly secret, he would have to tell her on his own.

What was she thinking? He wasn't the warrior of
the legend. He couldn't be. The man she knew was
flesh and blood and human emotion. But what about
the part of him she didn't know, the part he kept
hidden? Was there a side to him that showed itself
only in the still of night?

She walked numbly to the table and dropped
down into the chair. With a weary gesture she re-
moved the dark glasses and tossed them aside. She
no longer knew what to think or to believe.

It was still raining when John returned. The sound
of the door opening, the familiar vibration of his
footsteps, the rapid beating of her heart that invariably accompanied his return, brought Rennie to her
feet.

He sniffed the air. ''Let me guess. Willie Cypress
was here.''

She heard the rustling of paper bags.

''Give me a hand with these in the kitchen, would
you?''

She moved with a will that seemed to be outside

"I'd rather stay here tonight."

"You're not worried about that guy, are you? It isn't likely he'd find you in a little restaurant on the reservation."

This time it had nothing to do with Craig or being recognized. It had to do with there being a whole world out there that she wasn't sure she was prepared for, a world of mysticism and things that couldn't be explained. She felt safer right here within these walls. "No. I'm just feeling a little tired today, that's all."

"Okay," he said. "Maybe tomorrow. Willie must have talked your ears off. I don't blame you for wanting some peace and quiet."

There was something about the way she averted her gaze that should have warned him, but he was too busy admiring her eyes to notice. He was glad she no longer wore the dark glasses. Her eyes were clear and bright and as blue as the Everglades sky on a perfect spring day.

"What's this?" she asked, withdrawing an object from one of the bags.

"A flashlight. Hurricane season is here. I've got a weather radio for hurricane warnings. If one's coming, I'll get you out of here as fast as I can. But it never hurts to have an extra flashlight on hand."

He ripped open the pack of batteries he'd bought and inserted them into the flashlight. Flicking the button, he shone a ray of light around the room.

Rennie blinked several times. "What was that?"

coons, marsh rabbits and foxes foraging for food by the light of a rising moon. Her eyes were closed and she wasn't aware that John had finished making entries in his work journal, until a familiar sensation came over her and she knew without seeing that he was standing there before her.

Her breath quickened when he placed one knee on the edge of the mattress. She didn't see the smile on his full lips, but she felt his eyes, dark and intense, fixed on her. For the first time she was afraid. But of what? Of him? Or of herself, for wanting him in spite of what he might be?

His lips were gentle upon hers, as if he sensed her fear and sought to put it to rest. He breathed her name into her mouth, sending a spasm of pleasure through her. His hands began to search the swells and contours of her body, lingering on her breasts as if trapped by their softness.

She had never felt the kind of need she felt at this moment, not even in their previous lovemaking. There was something new tonight, an element of danger in the terrible knowledge she carried, which increased the pitch to a frightening frenzy. It had never been like this, and she couldn't bear to lose it. Take me! she wanted to scream.

He was stronger than she was, with sleek, hard muscles that should have warned her of the danger she was plunging into. But it didn't matter. Nothing mattered. When she was ready for him, she grasped

Chapter 10

Something awakened her.

She stirred and turned her head on the pillow. John was asleep beside her. She could feel the warmth of his breath on her face and smell the scent of the earth and the forest that lingered perpetually in his hair. She hadn't heard him come in last night, but even in slumber she had somehow known he was there, unconsciously moving into the embrace from which she had just awakened.

Careful not to wake him, she gently disentangled herself from his enveloping grasp and got up. She yawned, stretching her arms up over her head and walked barefoot to the door. Not knowing why or what awaited, she opened the door and stepped outside.

perfectly still, her heart thumping, tears threatening as the full impact was revealed to her.

All the words in the world could not describe the incredible beauty that unfolded before her newly found sight. She sucked in her breath with awe. The greenness all around was dazzling. The lush, tropical foliage was radiant, pristine and virtually unspoiled. Ribbons of purple and pink tinted a sapphire sky that stretched to the horizon. John was right. This place was paradise.

She was trembling, not from cold or fear, but from the sheer beauty that was all around her and from the exhilaration of the moment. Her eyes were wet with tears, as if she were seeing the world for the very first time. The breath inside of her stilled to a calmness she'd never felt before, and everything that had ever troubled her evaporated in the crystal-clear light that exploded over the treetops.

Her gaze swept the panorama. It was just as he had described it, only a hundred times more wonderful than anything she could have imagined. She felt a stab of regret knowing that it had been there all right under her nose while she'd been busy lying to herself about things that, in retrospect, didn't really matter.

Regaining her eyesight was like waking from a long, deep sleep and discovering an awareness of herself she never knew, like the connection she felt to this place even before its staggering beauty was revealed to her eyes. But with that insight came a

She closed her eyes in agony, blocking the pano-ramic beauty from her eyesight, though she could not chase it from her mind. How could she give all this up and return to a life that had been barren and without meaning?

She tried to look at the bright side. Now that she could see again, she could pursue her studies unhin-dered. With the revelation of the panther legend, who knew what other hidden truths lurked in Sem-inole myth? She tried to tell herself that the woman she had become in these past few weeks was stronger than the rich, pampered woman who had almost allowed herself to be pushed into a loveless marriage. But try as she might, she could not con-vince herself that going back was the right thing to do. Not when there was one major obstacle standing in her way.

John Panther.

Her breath quickened, not just from the tangled emotions that invariably accompanied the thought of him, but from the fear of the unknown. Last night, when she realized in the darkness that she loved him regardless of who or what he was, it had seemed so right. But today, with the world suddenly bathed in light, she wasn't so sure. Until now she'd been thrilled by the essence of him, but now she could not help but wonder what he looked like and what bearing, if any, it would have on her feelings for him. She wanted to believe herself capable of loving without regard to physical appeal, and it was the

cheekbones and straight nose, the uncertain smile on his lips that were full and finely etched. His face was a combination of beauty and roughness, with a level of strength in those features, something quiet and open, of immeasurable steadiness and patience.

The unexplained regret and remorse she heard all too often in his voice was there in the eyes that stared back at her. She wanted to go to him, to tell him that she knew what haunted him and that she loved him, anyway, but all she could do was stare at his handsome face and his lean, muscular body clad only in hastily pulled-on jeans, and think that in all her life she had never seen a more handsome man. Not handsome like the male models in men's clothing catalogs, with their classic features and perfect poses, but rather with an unrefined beauty of something rare and wild and dangerous. His rugged beauty was like a double-edged sword, on the one side the inexplicable allure of his nature that was filled with dark secrets, on the other side his formidable physical appearance making him different from any man she had ever known.

John knew by the way her eyes raced over him that she could see, and he steeled himself against the consequences. He stood rock still, forcing his skin not to quiver under the soft caress of her gaze. He felt himself stiffen as surely as if she had slipped her hand into his unzipped jeans. Somehow, he found his voice and asked tautly, "Disappointed?"

it's...it's...this. God, it's so beautiful. How can you stand it?''

''I know what you mean,'' he said. ''Not about the Easter egg, but about it being so beautiful that it almost hurts.''

She turned her head and looked at him. His gaze was fixed lovingly on the view. The barest smile lifted the corners of his lips. But as she watched, she saw a change come over him, almost imperceptible except for the subtle tensing of his jaw and the faint hardening of his smile.

''It's not all beautiful, though,'' he said solemnly. ''There's a lot of danger out there, and things that make you question who you are and why you do the things you do.''

He was thinking how everything from the past had led him to this moment. Suddenly he was filled with doubt as to which affected him the most, the killing of the panther that had caused him so much pain and sorrow or the woman standing beside him who made him feel things he thought he had buried with Maggie. For a reason he could not define, he knew that the two were somehow entwined.

Since the moment Rennie fell into his life, he was never afraid of the day she would see...until now. Could she read the fear in his eyes? Could she see past his defenses to the core of his aching heart? Did she know how afraid he was of loving her? Or worse, of her not loving him?

From the beginning he'd been impressed by her

did it to myself. After all, I had choices, but I squandered them just like my mother squandered hers. But unlike my mother, who did it for money, I did it for something far less attainable…love.

''I've spent a lifetime looking for love,'' she admitted, ''always thinking that maybe if I did it their way, just this once, they would love me for it. But they loved campaign parties more, and after years of looking, I learned not to expect it. Then came Craig, who offered love and security, or so I thought. Marrying him would have pleased the senator greatly, maybe even enough to glean a bit of affection out of him. I could kill two birds with one stone, and in the process, kill a bit of myself, as well.''

She was so honest about herself that it made John feel less than honorable. He wanted to tell her about the panther and what it was like for him. How he thought he was doomed to the same fate as the poor panther. How the prayer the warrior never said had, in a way, become his own prayer. And how the answer to that prayer was her. But the words froze on his tongue. What difference did any of it make, now that she had decided to leave? He didn't have to hear her say it. He could feel it crackling in the air. Speaking the words would only confirm what he already knew.

What right did he have to ask her to stay? This was his world, not hers. She might be happy here for a few days or weeks, until the novelty wore off.

"You mean the crash or the betrayal?" There was a ring of self-mockery in her tone.

"Both," he replied. "You're a survivor. Don't you get that about yourself?"

"There's a lot about myself I'm just beginning to learn," she admitted. "I have you to thank for that."

John's cheeks colored faintly and his dark lashes swooped down to hide his eyes. "I didn't make you who you are."

"No, but you saved my life. You also didn't send me packing. Either way, I wouldn't be here now."

"You also wouldn't be leaving."

There, he said them, the words that were sitting between them like unwanted company.

"You understand why I have to, don't you?"

"Sure," he said. "You have a life to get back to, with work and friends and..." His words trailed off awkwardly.

She looked at him. "And?"

He shrugged. "You know."

"No, I don't."

He felt like a kid who'd been caught doing something naughty and was being made to answer for it now. Trying hard to keep the jealousy out of his voice, he said, "That guy. The one you were going to marry."

Rennie's mouth fell open. "Craig?" She practically spat out the name. "I'd die before I'd ever go back to him."

She answered evasively, "I heard a few good ones."

"Too bad you didn't get the one you really wanted."

Oh, but she had. But she figured that by the time John found out from old Willie Cypress that she had, she'd be long gone, sparing him any embarrassment. Because if he knew that she knew, he would surely ask her if she believed it, and she would have to tell him that, yes, not only did she believe it, but she believed it of him.

"You can't always get what you want," she said.

John quipped, "Isn't that a song by the Rolling Stones?"

Rennie nodded, smiling to herself. Every time she imagined him as something primitive and wild, he surprised her by reminding her how he wasn't all that different from anybody else who liked chicken noodle soup, literature and rock and roll. But he wasn't simply a man like any other man, she reminded herself. It was that dissimilarity—the darkness combined with his sameness—that made him so unique. To her he was part legend and part reality, living an almost wild existence in a wild and unforgiving place, yet also civilized in ways most men weren't. She knew she would never meet another man like him, and it made leaving him that much more unbearable.

All he had to do was ask her to stay and she would have agreed in a heartbeat, but the words she

The kind of lovemaking that's heated and quick and fills a desperate momentary need.

Despite his arousal, however, he made no move toward her. Tonight he decided. He would wait until the moon was high. After he returned from his nocturnal hunt, he would lie down next to her and awaken her with his caresses. That was invariably the time when he needed her the most, and when she would be most receptive to his advances. He liked the thought of waking her up that way. Her body would be warm with sleep and open easily to him, and he could lose himself in her and remember what it was like to be an ordinary man again, when the thing that mattered most was no further away than the woman beneath him. And he wanted this woman beneath him, not for a night, but for more, so much more that it scared him. He got to his feet and stood towering over her, trying to maintain a hold on his emotions.

Rennie looked up at him. Never had his six-foot frame seemed as ominous as it did at this very moment. His dark eyes moved over her with the intensity of a man with something on his mind. The bulge in his jeans made his intention clear. He had the look about him of a creature that was about to pounce.

Her heart fluttered wildly with anticipation, then sank with disappointment when he made no move to take her. Instead, he just stood there devouring her with his eyes for what seemed like an eternity. In reality it was only seconds, but there was some-

Chapter 11

It was an elegantly appointed room. A mahogany bookcase engulfed one entire wall from floor to ceiling, holding a leather-bound law library. A studded burgundy leather chesterfield flanked by matching leather wing chairs sat atop an antique Aubusson carpet. The lower half of the walls was paneled in teak from East India, above was painted a deep crimson. A large glass-and-chrome desk stood before the arched windows with the scores of leaded panes, looking stark and powerful against the warm, deep tones of the room, much the way the senator exerted his own stark and powerful persona on those around him.

Rennie had been in this room countless times and it never ceased to chill her. No matter how many

eyes were vacant, the mouth unsmiling. Rennie felt a pang of love and regret as she looked at the picture of her mother. Despite all the things that money could buy, her mother had been the unhappy, unfulfilled wife of Senator Trevor Hollander, a role she despised but which she played with Academy Award-winning persuasiveness. With a sigh Rennie looked away, wondering how it was possible to love someone she had never really liked.

Instead of the usual childhood photograph of a child sitting on a pony at the zoo, there was Rennie at age nine astride her own Arabian mare at an equestrian event. The funny thing was, she'd been afraid of horses as a child. But the senator, knowing her fear, was determined that she get over it by enrolling her in every junior equestrian event his country club sponsored. She eventually did get over her fear of horses, but only because she discovered that the barn was a safe place to hide from the senator's overbearing influence and her mother's obsequious behavior, and that the horses, who made no demands on her and didn't judge her, were her real family.

The photograph looked foreign to her, the face of the little girl who had been her like the face of a stranger, the memories of that part of her life distant. But it wasn't just the passage of years or the growing up that made her feel different. Everything was different. *She* was different.

The weeks she'd been away felt like years. There were no bridges left to the past, nothing to connect

who, Rennie had learned many years go, had an on-going affair with him. It was her mother who told her about it, confiding her relief that at least the senator had someone who could take care of *those things* for him so that she didn't have to.

He sat down on the leather couch. Others looked lost in the expanse of top-grain leather, but not him. Like everything else in his life, he dominated it.

"So, Renata, where did that job of yours take you these past few weeks?"

"Profession," she corrected without answering. "It's a *profession.*"

He crossed one leg casually over the other, although Rennie knew there was nothing casual about him. Every movement, every gesture was carefully orchestrated to convey an impression of superiority and impatience, as evidenced now by the drumming of his fingers on the rolled arm of the sofa.

"Did you do something different with your hair?" he inquired.

So, he did notice something different about her. She was glad that he could only make a lame guess as to what it was, and experienced a momentary private triumph knowing that it was her secret and he had no control over it.

"No," she answered.

"So are you going to finally explain to me why I got a call one day informing me that your plane went off radar and couldn't be accounted for?"

"There was a slight accident with the plane. It's

think we brought in something like two hundred and fifty thousand.''

"That must be small change compared to what the insurance lobby contributes," she said. "I heard that a patients' bill of rights was on the floor. Did you vote it down again?"

"You're damn right I did. You give people the right to sue their HMOs and medical malpractice will skyrocket."

Rennie put her hand up before he went off on one of his tangents. "I didn't come here to debate political issues with you."

"I thought not. So, are you going to tell me why you did come, or must I pull it out of you?"

She bristled at the disdainful tone of his voice. "It's about Craig."

"Ah, yes, the jilted fiancé. I was wondering when you would get around to that."

"You heard?" It was more of a statement than a question.

"Of course I heard. Did you think he was going to just go away quietly?"

"I don't care what he does. He doesn't want me. He wants—"

"What any ambitious man wants," the senator interrupted. "And what right have you to deny him?"

"I'm not denying Craig Wolfson anything. He can have whatever he wants. He just can't have me."

She turned away from the distasteful smell of the cigar. It wasn't so much that he found countless ways to excuse Craig's controlling behavior that annoyed her. Both men were, after all, cut from the same cloth of unscrupulous ambition. It was just that he seemed too eager to pin the blame on her.

"Charity work at the ladies' guild?" she said sarcastically. "I don't think so."

"Perhaps if you spoke to him and explained your position."

If bullying tactics didn't work, he generally resorted to calm persuasion. She'd seen his act a hundred times and knew it well.

"It's not only me he manipulated," she told him. "It was you, also."

"Oh? How so?"

"Craig was only going to marry me to get that piece of real estate you promised him as a wedding gift. He never loved me. I heard him say so."

"You must have misunderstood."

Behind the thin veil of smoke he looked detached and remote, the way Craig had looked that night as he had stood at his desk smoking the same brand of cigar.

Rennie waved away the smoke that drifted to where she was standing. "Where'd you get those things? And don't tell me from Castro."

"They were a gift from Craig," he replied.

It wasn't surprising. A gift of expensive Cuban cigars was but one way Craig curried the senator's

if he even let you keep your position at the university. Money is what makes a good marriage, not love. Frankly, Renata, after having been used to fine things your whole life, I don't see you living in a shack somewhere with some brooding hulk of a man who in his whole life will never earn what Craig Wolfson earns in a single year. Tell me, dear, where's the love when the money runs out?''

His unwitting mockery of the very situation she'd spent the past several weeks in rendered Renata speechless. Even as only part human, John Panther was more of a man than Craig Wolfson could ever hope to be. But she couldn't tell the senator that. John Panther was a secret she'd never share with anyone, least of all him.

In the same tone he used with assistants and servants, he continued, ''Now, this is what you're going to do. You will telephone Craig and tell him you're sorry for breaking the engagement. You've thought it over and you've realized you were wrong. Don't worry about him taking you back. I've spoken to him and he's perfectly amenable, provided, of course, that you understand the, shall we say, terms of the arrangement.''

''Which are?''

He replied with terse simplicity, ''You marry Craig. Craig gets the land.''

''But—''

His voice overrode her accusingly. ''You were always idealistic and naïve. Not only in your chosen

His face mottled with fury, but she didn't care. It was time to set the record straight, and to hell with the consequences.

"For your information, I'm not my mother. I don't worship money. I can live without it. And unlike her, I'd never marry without love."

They were words too long left unspoken, festering like a wound she thought would never heal. Until she met a man whose wounds were deeper than her own and who gave her the courage to begin the painful healing process. Her face flushed with anger, she felt a staggering rush of relief as the words, like an infection, poured out.

"Furthermore, you're not my father."

Perhaps if she had seen a flash of hurt in his eyes, or the merest flinching of a muscle on his face telling her that she had wounded him, she would have said no more. But those features fixed in cold disdain told her with cruel certainty that he had never loved her enough to be hurt by her.

"I'm under no obligation to do anything you say, and that includes marrying a despicable worm like Craig Wolfson. If you like him so much, you marry him!"

She stormed out, slamming the door on him and on that part of her life.

Later that night, at home alone in her condo, she was unable to sleep, feeling angry, confused and guilty. She'd never forgive him for his part in the conspiracy to marry her off to a man she didn't love,

She knew only that for the first time in her life she was deeply and desperately in love. But what about John Panther? Deep in his soul, was he even capable of love?

The road snaked north toward the Big Cypress Reservation through sighing saw grass and low-lying pastures where cattle crowded shoulder-deep in the tall grass. The land rose dark green from the softness of the Everglades, and although the orange trees stood in regimental rows and the road curved past modern houses and a shiny new school, there was a wild feel to the place, like the stubborn independence that filled John's heart.

But even at Big Cypress, miles away from anywhere, the outside world encroached. Mistrust of the white world had been part of Seminole culture and history for years, and here he was, pining for a white woman as if he had learned nothing at all.

She was the reason he was driving to the reservation. He had to get away from that cabin where memories of her lingered in every corner or he'd go mad. The place that had been his refuge for more than a year and a half felt like a coffin, smothering him with its closeness and isolation. It reached a point where the sound of no one answering every time he spoke was more than he could bear. By day he was doomed by her memory that would not go away. At night he was haunted by dreams of her. He would awaken in a sweat and reach for her, but

said softly. "Your wife." She left the name unspoken out of respect for the dead. "And now this white woman."

Anger sharpened his tone. "Are you saying I should be used to it?"

"I am saying that you cannot live your life without pain. It's how you deal with the pain that makes you who you are. I have never known you to crumble under it or to let it stop you from doing what you feel in your heart you must do."

She had never approved of his decision to go after the panther, warning him on numerous occasions that it could only lead to trouble. But he suspected that her meaning now had nothing to do with the panther. He looked hard into her ebony eyes. "You're not telling me to go after her, are you?"

Lorena had witnessed firsthand the white man's influence on their people, but she was, after all, his mother, and she could not stand by and watch him suffer just for loving someone, even if that someone was white. She also knew how difficult it had always been for him to reconcile his emotions.

"You must do the thing you think you cannot do."

The words were familiar. All his life, this brave, intelligent woman had encouraged him to go beyond the bounds he set for himself, to challenge the world around him, Seminole and white, and to answer only to his inner self. He knew what she was telling him now. He had to put his fear aside and go after the

His head whipped up at that, one dark lock of hair slicing across his face. "Love? Tell me what woman would love a man who cannot protect her."

Lorena looked at him incredulously. "From what? The panther?"

"I can blame it on the panther for the rest of my life, but I know in my heart that's the coward's way out. No, mother, I meant from myself."

She knew he'd been deeply hurt by his wife's death and the terrible load of shame he carried over it. But until now she had not truly understood the depth of that pain, nor the extent of the blame he placed upon himself.

"The panther killed Maggie because of *me*. Because *I* couldn't protect her. Because of *my* stupidity. I should have known from the legend what can happen when you hunt for a reason that's not true."

"The panthers are disappearing," she said. "You were only trying to help."

His voice rose above the urgent plea in hers. "Don't you see? I should have left them alone!"

Lorena's fingers tightened around his forearm. Harshly she admonished, "If it was the Spirit Being's will that you be the one to aid His children, the panthers, who are you to question it? And if it is His will that you are to love again, who are you to doubt it? Put that arrogance away. It has no place in a Seminole's heart."

His mother's shaming words hit John hard. She was right. It was arrogant of him to assume that he

Chapter 12

With an absentminded tug, Rennie pulled the sash of her satin robe tighter around her waist and pushed back the tousled hair that fell into her eyes as she made her way into the kitchen.

She put a kettle of water on the burner and dropped two slices of bread into the toaster. Gone was her appetite for anything more elaborate in the morning than toast and coffee. And even that seemed somehow purposeless to her.

If she had been going through the motions of living before, then the way she was living now was worse. Before, she did it without knowing why she was doing it, or even that she was doing it. Living outside of herself was the norm—until her plane had crashed and her inner world had exploded. She still knew he wanted her. He proved just how much the night before she left. The other times it had been breathtaking and exciting and frightening all at once. But that night, making love with him by the light of the moon that came in through the window, feeling, and finally being able to see, the raw power of him, was even more thrilling, even more frightening because it had been goodbye, and they both knew it.

Never before had she felt so completely taken, so filled by his desperate desire. But she knew that desire and love were two separate things. That he desired her was indisputable. But what about love? Could she live with one and not the other?

There was no denying the passion that raged between them. But animal desire was not enough. Once, what seemed like a long time ago, the person she was then might have been willing to settle for only that. But the woman she was now would not. Making love with him would always leave her breathless, but she would always long for more, and he would be unable to give it. No, it was for the best that she left, so that he could get on with the tragic consequences of his life, and she could get on with what was left of hers.

She turned the hot water on in the shower and slipped out of her robe. It was funny how things that were previously so ritualistic now seemed out of character. She held her hand beneath the stream of water. Even that felt oddly out of sync. While the water was heating up, she went back into the bed-

sad reality. What kind of life would they have had if she'd stayed? The answer was painful and invariably the same. It would have been a life in which a large part of the time she would have been without him. By day he would have belonged to her and she to him. By night she would be alone, while he lived out his cruel destiny. Children? How could she bring his child into this world knowing that it might suffer the same fate as its father? And yet in spite of every obstacle she could imagine, the sad and simple truth was that she would have stayed despite all the odds if only he had told her that he loved her.

A terrible loneliness engulfed her. It wasn't just the wistful yearning for something undefined. It was an acute longing for some*one*. For John. For the hard, driving strength of his body filling hers. How ironic it was that the very thing she loved most was the reason she could never go back.

A hot shower did little to ease Rennie's pain. But then, this was hardly a case of sore muscles. This was a suffering that went much deeper, past muscle and tendon, to the very fibers of her heart that loved him beyond all doubt and reason.

After her shower the mirror above the sink squeaked when she ran her hand over it to erase the steam. She bent over from the waist and began to dry her hair with a towel, when a knock on the door brought her head up sharply, sending droplets of water flying into the air from the ends of her still-wet hair. Her thoughts screeched to a halt. Oh, God, she

a cab to take you home.'' His face retained its stoic expression, but his coal-dark eyes moved over her with the intensity of a hungry man. She looked utterly provocative in a peach-colored satin robe that kept slipping off one shoulder. She smelled fresh and intoxicating from her shower, her tawny hair curling in damp, undisciplined waves around her face.

His gaze returned to her face that was pale and beautiful. ''Who'd you think it was?''

Rennie felt herself heating up under John's stare. Nervously she drew the robe tighter around her body, unaware that doing so only made the curve of her hips and the swell of her breasts even more obvious to him. She answered honestly, ''Craig. I had it out with my stepfather last night and I figured he'd heard about it.''

''Do you think he'll come?''

She shrugged and the robe slipped again off her shoulder. Aware that his eyes were on her, she hastily pushed it back up. ''Hopefully I'll be gone by then.''

Something flashed in his dark eyes. ''Where are you going?''

''I don't know. Anywhere. Just not here.''

''You're not afraid of him, are you?''

Not since loving you gave me the courage to fear nothing, she thought. But that was only partly true. The thing was, she felt uncomfortable here. This

I think, cleared the way for a better understanding between us. If Craig calls, I'll tell him to go to hell, and that will be that."

He gave a derisive little snort and said, "It's great that you can tie things up so neatly like that."

"What do you expect me to do?"

Come back. Be with me. Help me to get past the pain. "Whatever you feel in your heart is right."

Why was he making this harder than it had to be? Why couldn't he just let her nurse her broken heart in private? Didn't he know that seeing him again only made it worse? "Why did you come here."

"I told you."

"You told me what you're telling yourself."

He shook his head with frustration. "I could give you a thousand reasons for my coming, and they'd all be lies."

"Then why don't you try the truth? You do know what that is, don't you, John?"

He answered haltingly, "It's not that easy."

"Why?"

John expelled a long, deep breath that had been trapped in his lungs for what seemed like forever. Because I've seen things and done things I can't tell you about. Because I want you so much, not just now, this moment, for tomorrow and all the tomorrows after that, and it scares me.

His silence, and the look of uncharacteristic helplessness on his face, was all the answer she needed. "It's all right," she said. "I know about it."

would make it so. You cling to the hope that you're not the thing you really are.''

She came closer, but not so close that he could reach out and touch her. If he touched her, she'd be lost to all reason. ''This thing you are,'' she said, her voice barely a whisper, ''I can't even imagine how terrible it must be, living by day as a man, by night as...'' He was right. It was harder to say than she thought it would be. ''...as...something else.''

''Something else?'' The surprise was evident in his tone. His ebony eyes narrowed as he looked at her. ''What are you talking about?''

Rennie bit her lip. There was no turning back. ''The panther, John, I know it's you. But it doesn't matter, at least not to me.''

She went to the window where she stood silhouetted against the sunlight, looking out at the water. ''It doesn't matter. I love you, anyway.'' She held her breath for his reply, but when her confession was greeted by stony silence, she turned back to him, and with matter-of-fact resignation, said, ''It's true. I'm in love with you, John. I know what you are, and I love you, anyway.''

John took a staggering step backward as an army of emotions converged on him. So, she didn't know the truth about him after all. But what she knew, or thought she knew, was so much worse that it stunned him. He found the idea of her love startling. Were it not for the look of utter truth in her eyes, he never would have believed her.

me back. I know from experience that you can't
make somebody love you.''

He took a step toward her and stopped, not daring
to get any closer for fear that an even more basic
instinct would get the better of him. ''You asked me
before why I came here. It was to tell you something
about myself.''

''I know you didn't want me to find out,'' she
said, ''but now that I have, are you going to deny
it? Are you going to tell me that you don't carry a
terrible secret inside of you?''

''No, I'm not going to tell you that. I do carry a
secret, Rennie, but it's not what you think it is. In
some ways, it's worse. That poor warrior acted without thinking. My sin is that I knew what I was doing,
and I did it, anyway.''

She looked at him with a blank expression, her
brows knit delicately with confusion.

''I'm not him, Rennie. I'm not the warrior of the
legend.'' He took a deep breath, held it for an in-
determinate moment in which his whole life seemed
to hang in midair, and let it out slowly. ''There's
something I have to tell you, and after you hear it,
if you decide that you don't love me, I'll understand.''

He walked to the sofa and sat down with his elbows on his knees, head in hands. For many long
minutes he said nothing as he gathered his thoughts
and emotions and searched for a way to begin. He
was tired. It wasn't the bone tired that came from a

ness. Seeing it mirrored in the dark eyes that looked up at her made Rennie realize how much a part of him his vengeance was. She turned back to the window in anguish, saying nothing.

The water was unusually bright, the sky uncommonly blue. Twenty-one floors below people went about their business. It was hard to imagine life going on as usual when her own life was falling apart around her, for discovering that John was not the half man, half animal creature that wandered the swamp only deepened Rennie's agony. Was his guilt over his wife's death, and his obsession with killing the panther the only things that mattered to him? Where did she fit into his life?

A great chasm of silence filled the room. Rennie was no longer sure where John's suffering ended and hers began. But she did know one thing. She owed him an apology for thinking he was less than human. If there was any doubt of it before, there was none now. Only a human heart could hurt as much as this one was hurting.

She was standing before him in her bare feet. He commanded himself to look at her, to see once and for all if what he feared the most was written in her eyes. Slowly, haltingly, his gaze came up to meet hers. But there was no hatred, no disgust or shame raining down on his from her blue eyes.

She sat down beside him and placed a soft white hand upon his, drawing it up from his lap and touch-

can you know me so well, as I know in my heart that you do, and have such little faith in me?''

He let the fabric slip from his fingers. This, he was discovering, was an even greater torment than the one he'd known before. This woman loved him. He saw it in her eyes, bright with tears, and heard it in her softly beseeching voice. She loved him. But it wasn't as simple as that. How could he give her the complete and committed love she deserved when he had unfinished business to take care of?

''After I do what I have to do,'' he muttered. ''Maybe then.''

Rennie drew back with the soft gasp of disbelief. ''You're still going after him?''

The dark eyes which only moments ago had caressed her face now flashed with steely determination. ''Nothing's changed in that regard. He's out there and I'm going to find him. And then—'' He shrugged his broad shoulders fatalistically. ''I guess we'll see, won't we?''

She was hurt, and he knew it. ''Please understand, Rennie,'' he implored.

Stiffly she replied, ''I understand perfectly. Some things are just more important than others.''

He wanted to take her in his arms and show her just how important she was to his very being, but he knew she wouldn't have let him, not now. What was the point of telling her? he bitterly asked himself. He'd told her the truth, and now there was a distance between them even wider than before.

In a lightning-quick move his hand shot out and clamped down hard over Rennie's forearm, fingers squeezing tight. He knew he was hurting her, but he had to get her attention. He had to make her understand.

In a tightly controlled voice, through gritted teeth he said, "Don't you see? If I can't reconcile the past, there is no future. Not for me. If what I feel for you is to have any chance at all, I have to go back. I have to settle the score."

Stubbornly clinging to his vendetta against the panther, John dropped his hand and walked to the door, leaving Rennie heartbroken that he would sacrifice their chance of happiness, the flesh on her arm still bearing red marks from where his fingers had bitten into it long after he was gone.

The Seminoles hadn't lost their culture. They were just living a different kind of culture, one that, out of necessity, included the white world and everything that came with it.

It was easier for the old-timers at Brighton and Big Cypress, with their isolation, harder at the reservation in Hollywood where young Seminoles were essentially city kids. For John, it wasn't the money or the material things the white world offered that had an impact on his life. What need did he have for any of that, when this untamed wilderness teeming with life and with memories was all that really mattered?

Yet, what the white world offered him was even harder to ignore, much less deny. It had brought him a remarkable woman, a woman any man would have been proud to call his own. Any man, that is, except him. There was no pride in hearing a woman tell you she loved you, and then walking away from her.

He'd seen the acute pain in her blue eyes just before he turned and walked out the door, and as much as it had affected him, it hadn't dissuaded him from doing what he knew in his heart he had to do. What she didn't know was that the pain he was suffering over it was as great as her own…maybe even greater, considering that he'd already lost so much and now stood to lose even more.

Losing the things that mattered most to him was becoming a habit he deplored. If it was the last thing he did, he would find that cat and kill it. Hopefully,

turn on the light. He had returned only to collect his pack and go back out again. He'd made up his mind. He was going after the panther tonight, and he wasn't coming back until he'd finished what he set out to do. There was nothing left to lose.

"Going somewhere?"

A familiar voice spoke from the darkness, freezing John in midmotion as he reached for his backpack. Everything inside of him tensed. His head whirled in her direction, the violence of the movement whipping the dark hair off his face.

Even in the darkness she was beautiful, and he was powerless to stop himself from wanting her, a gut reaction since the day she fell into his life. He snatched his backpack off the table and said roughly, "I hope you didn't come to try and talk me out of it. It won't work. My mind's made up."

She spoke from the shadows. "I know it is."

When he walked out of her condo that day, leaving marks on her arm and inflicting a wound on her heart, Rennie had thought she would die. She had cried herself to sleep, lamenting her inability to get through to him. If only she'd been able to change his mind. If only... But come morning, all the if-onlys in the world made no difference. His past was a part of him. The death of his wife. His grief over it. Even his insane obsession with the panther. It molded him into the man he was today, the man she fell in love with. Morning shed light on the indis-

strictly anthropological standpoint. From a purely personal perspective, however, her reasons were entirely different. For the first time in her life a man wanted her not for her money or her family connection but for herself. It made her feel wanted...necessary. This, she knew with all certainty, was her missing link, and now that she had found it, she wasn't about to let it go without a fight.

"When you catch it, will you—"

"Kill it," he said abruptly. "Do you have a problem with that?"

Who was she to judge him, when her own life had been in such utter disarray before she met him? His strength and gentle caring had enabled her to put things in order, to make sense out of who she was and what she wanted. In truth, she loved him as much for his intelligence and strength as she did for this one weakness, for in it she recognized the aching and vulnerable heart of the hunter.

"What are we waiting for?" she asked.

The morning broke bright and clear and unbearably hot. Breakfast was a collaboration of scrambled eggs and bacon that John made and the coffee that Rennie made. Sitting on a fallen log, John took one sip and grimaced. "Where'd you learn to make coffee?" he complained, tossing what was left in his cup into the bushes.

He'd been edgy and abrasive since they set out. It was obvious he didn't want her there. He made a

find his way out of his dark mood just as he found his way through the swamp.

About midday they stopped to rest. John got down into the knee-deep water. He made no move to place his hands about her waist and lift her down as he'd always done before, so Rennie climbed down into the water and did her best to slog through the muddy bottom that sucked at her feet as she waded to shore.

With Rennie sitting in the shade beneath a tree, John searched the area for a stick that would suit his purpose. Finding one, he quickly carved the tip into a point, and returned with it to the water, where he speared a fish. Back on shore, he cleaned and gutted it and tossed it into a frying pan over a small fire he'd got going.

He passed some to Rennie on a paper plate. "You'd better sit in the sun if you want to dry out." His deep voice broke the silence that had been sitting between them all morning like an unwelcome guest.

Rennie's jeans were wet from midthigh down, but although the denim was heavy from the water it had absorbed, the wetness was a cool relief to the stagnant heat that swelled all around them as the day heated up. From where she sat with her back against the trunk of a tree, she nibbled on the fish and observed him.

Droplets of perspiration glided down the sides of his handsome face, glistening in the sunlight. He looked ominous, but she knew by the sound of his

about to say something, when the words caught in his throat. A ray of yellow sunlight slashed through the trees and danced in her hair. She looked so beautiful, so fair and sparkling next to his own skin and dark demeanor, and the difference between them had never been so acute as it was at this moment. That a woman like her could love a man like him stilled whatever harsh words he'd been about to utter.

He forced his gaze away before he did something stupid like go over there and kiss her. That would certainly take the edge off, but in this deadly game of cat and mouse, it was precisely that edge he needed.

"There's a population of about forty adults centered mainly in Collier and Hendry counties," he said. "That's the only population that remains that we know of anywhere. If there's a panther in this area, it's alone and it's him."

"What do you want me to do?" she asked.

"You? Nothing. This is my fight, Rennie. I'll handle it."

"I won't be dismissed that easily," she objected.

He answered dryly, "I noticed."

He knew he was crazy for bringing her with him on such a dangerous adventure, but seeing her unexpectedly at the cabin, with moonlight slanting across her face, he'd been powerless to deny her. The dismal fact was that he wanted her with him. Not just her body, although he craved that as surely

the power to take it all away from him as it had done before. "Get your things," he barked. "It's time to go."

They continued their journey in wordless unease. When dusk fell, they found a spot along the bank and set up camp for the night.

Twilight played in soft shadows over the hammock in which they were camped. The summer sky flashed a flickering finale to the day. Soon the full face of the moon shone down on them from an ebony sky strewn with stars that glittered like diamonds.

The air crackled from the small campfire John made that sent yellow sparks into the night and cast warm shadows over Rennie's face as she sat cross-legged on a bed of moss and leaves.

Earlier she had watched him catch and kill a rabbit. As its meat browned now on a spit over the open flames, she recalled the shudder that had gone through her at the sight of it. There had been no malice to it, no hostility. It had been the simple, matter-of-fact action of a man catching food the way his ancestors had done. She had watched wordlessly as he paused over the animal's lifeless body, his lips moving in a prayer not meant for her ears. The impact of his Indianness had never been greater than it had been at that moment.

When he offered her a bit of his kill, she refused, choosing instead to munch on a chocolate bar she had in her bag. It wasn't that she was squeamish

what he was, a man who had made a dreadful mistake and was having a hard time living with it. But that was before Rennie. Now the darkness reeked of loneliness and emptiness.

His low voice carried across the space between them. "I don't expect you to understand why I have to do this."

"Does it matter whether or not I do?" she replied.

Yes, he thought, it did. More than he wanted to admit. "He and I have a score to settle."

"What if you never catch him?"

His gaze dropped, and he plucked absentmindedly at the blades of grass. The thought of going on like this, lost and alone, without ever catching the panther and putting an end to it, was a possibility John had never allowed himself to consider...until now. If he didn't end this thing once and for all, the anger and the guilt would eat him up inside and he would lose himself...and Rennie...forever. "I'll catch him," he vowed.

That was precisely what Rennie was afraid of, that John would catch and kill the panther, only to find that it didn't bring the salvation he hoped for. If that happened, it would only lock him further into his grief and guilt and shut him away from her forever.

A deep, guttural sound tore through the stillness of the night, carrying a more imperative fear. "Wh-what's that?" Rennie asked in a muffled gasp.

"Bull alligator," John replied.

welled up within him to a terrible crescendo. In one swift move she was beneath him. The air filled with the fragrance of the soft green grass crushed at her back. His hands tore at the buttons of her shirt to expose her flesh to the warm summer night. Roughly he caught her bottom lip between his teeth and drew it into his mouth, sucking and nibbling and forcing little gasping moans from her. In the next dizzying moment he released it and brought his open mouth down again on hers, this time to draw the breath right out of her lungs and into his being.

He was drowning, sinking deeper into an ocean of such longing and desire that the only thing keeping him alive at this moment was her sweet breath filling him.

When he entered her, it was like coming home to the place where he belonged. In this sanctuary, for these precious few minutes, the perilous quest he had set for himself was all but forgotten.

life other than Rennie's quiet breathing as she slept and his own, which stilled now as he listened to the static silence all around them.

He glanced at the woman sleeping with her head against his shoulder, innocent of the danger that lurked in the darkness. Again he cursed his foolish decision to let her come along. Gently he slipped his arm from beneath her head. His hand slid slowly across the ground to the spot where he'd left his knife. His fingers searched for the weapon, made crucial contact, closed tightly around the hilt and drew it close.

There was a presence in the still night air. Into John's nostrils wafted a warm-blooded, musty smell. Without a sound he rose to his feet, relying on his intellect and his senses to tell him what he already knew.

"Rennie, wake up."

It wasn't so much his whisper as the urgency in it that awakened her. She opened her eyes to the sight of John towering over her. He was fully dressed. In his hand he clutched a knife.

Sleep vanished instantly from Rennie's eyes. She opened her mouth to speak, but his hand shot up to silence her. Suddenly she was afraid.

He motioned for her to get dressed. She obeyed, rising wordlessly and slipping back into her clothes with trembling hands, her heart pounding so loudly in her ears she was sure it could be heard into the deepest recesses of the swamp.

face, and Rennie winced from the pain of them as sharply as if he had struck her. Weakly she asked, "What about us?"

What could he say? That there was no *us* while this thing loomed over him? Why was she making this harder than it had to be? "Why are you in my life. Why, dammit?"

"Because I love you."

"Love won't help me catch that bastard."

He was trying to hurt her and succeeding. Tears streamed down Rennie's cheeks. "No, it won't. But love can mend a broken heart if only you'll let it."

"You can't mend something that broke into a million pieces a long time ago," he said resolutely.

She took a faltering step backward as his words hit home. She barely managed to choke out the words. "And what about me?"

John drew the night air deeply into his lungs and let it out in a breath of self-disgust. "I don't know what I feel anymore."

Inside, Rennie was dying. Everything she had feared the most was coming true. She felt suddenly foolish and naïve for having believed this dark and complex man capable of the simplest human emotion. She wished the ground would open and swallow her up and she wouldn't have to see that look on his face that told her she didn't matter.

One more dream was shattered. But unlike the other times, when she had given in to the pain, this time something inside of her hardened like steel. She

great that she sank to her knees in the grass and wept from the pain of it.

The cover of night proved no obstacle to John's keen eyesight, and it wasn't hard to pick up the panther's tracks.

The cat made its way across a grassy hammock, leaving prints in the softly tamped earth. It was hunting for a mole or a rabbit to satisfy its hunger, unaware of the man who followed relentlessly behind.

John knelt on one knee to silently and deftly assemble his traps. He had hoped for a breeze so that he could position himself downwind and escape detection by the panther's keen sense of smell. But the air was still and heavy, with not a leaf stirring. The cat was sure to catch his scent. He'd have to rely on the cat's hunger.

From his bag he produced a slice of leftover rabbit, which he cut into small pieces and placed around the perimeter of the area. Panthers, he knew, were opportunistic hunters and not about to pass up an easy meal.

With his traps set and his knife in his hand, he crouched down among the scrub brush to wait. He was oblivious to the sweat that snaked down the sides of his face to dot his shoulders with wetness. Overhead the stars had disappeared and a funnel of clouds obscured the sky. It was going to rain, not just the patter of a spring shower, but a full-blown summer thunderstorm. Mosquitoes buzzed madden-

He thought of his mother, who had raised him to be fiercely self-sufficient, not only in his environment, but in his thoughts. Despite her disapproval of the path of exile and retribution he had chosen for himself, she never ceased believing in the goodness that she claimed was still in him.

He could not think of the women in his life without thinking of the one who had crash-landed in his heart.

Only now, sitting in the dense stillness, with nothing around him except his thoughts and regrets, did he realize what Rennie had said. She had asked him to have pity on the panther because of the very thing it was. Part man, part animal, isn't that what she'd said? In that simple, matter-of-fact statement was a belief that defied all logic. But what shocked him the most was that, unlike himself, born and raised with the Seminole myths and legends burned strongly into his spirit, Rennie chose consciously to believe in something another outsider would have thought unbelievable.

She was an extraordinary woman, unwittingly courageous in ways he was not, touching something inside of him that went far beyond the physical. He had always assumed that with the capture and death of the panther the past would be behind him forever. But now he wasn't so sure. Rennie had instilled a measure of doubt in him by giving him a glimpse of something far more fulfilling than the quenching of his thirst for revenge. With her acceptance of the

When Maggie died, he thought all the love went out of him and would never return, but Rennie brought it back. The unconditional love she offered brought a sense of wholeness. And with that wholeness came freedom.

Suddenly Rennie's words echoed sharply through his mind. "What if you never catch him?" Only now, with hour stretching upon lonely hour, did he consider it for the very first time. And only now did he ask himself if it really mattered.

For the warrior of the legend his fate was sealed because of a prayer not spoken. For John the answer to his unspoken prayer was Rennie. She came into his life at a time when he was ready to let go, only he hadn't realized it. Her love showed him the way, and he swore now that he would find her, when his work here was finished, and tell her how much he loved her for it.

The soft brush of something large moving through the undergrowth brought John's thoughts screeching to a halt.

With all his senses attuned, he tracked the movements of the panther until it came into view.

It was a big mature male, an easy hundred pounds of pure stealth and muscle. Lured by the scent of food, unmindful of the pouring rain, he approached cautiously, picking his way through puddles of mud that formed in the grass.

He had not fed in days. Unlike its human counterpart, whose skill at hunting by day was aided by

under which she had sought shelter during the night. The heat rose above the wet ground in steamy tatters, giving a hazy, unreal look to everything it touched. The air resonated with the sounds of bullfrogs, insects humming, birds awakening to greet a new day.

She loved this time of day, especially here in the Everglades. Above, traces of night still lingered in the sky that glowed sapphire in places. The air was hot, but it was clear and clean and carried the moist, green scent of the swamp.

She was tired, her body aching from a sleepless night. But more than that, she felt alone. She had hoped the dawn would bring with it that same handsome face that stole her breath away, but when he failed to return by late morning, her hope began to dim. Where was he? Why wasn't he back by now? Had something terrible happened?

Rennie didn't know if she should stay or go. Whatever happened to him out there, she couldn't bear the thought of not being there when, and if, he returned. Victorious or not, she had to see his face.

She was even willing to let herself believe that with the killing of the panther she had a chance to win his love. After all, there were no guarantees in life, and a man like John Panther was worth risking everything for. Before, she had dreaded the possibility of him catching the panther. Now she dreaded the possibility that he didn't.

him, but something stopped her. She searched his face, but found only an unreadable look fixed on those handsome features. Had he failed? Her heart wept for him and for herself.

He walked into the clearing. "I thought you would have been back at the cabin by now."

There was no anger in his tone, no disillusionment. Nevertheless, it was with icy caution that she replied, "I was just about to call Willie."

He couldn't blame her for being angry with him for not returning last night. He glanced at the bed of leaves she had gathered beneath the branches. The thought of Rennie alone out here was not a pleasant one.

"Forget the call," he said. "Why don't you help me gather some firewood for tonight instead? I figured we'd spend another night here before heading back in the morning."

Rennie glared back at him incredulously. "Another night? Here?"

He shrugged haphazardly. "Why not?"

She stormed up to him then. "I'll tell you why not. Because you're out of your mind if you think I'm going to spend another night out here alone while you race off after that damned cat."

"Well, actually—" he began.

"Never mind," she said heatedly. "If you want to stay and continue this vendetta, you can do it without me. I don't know, John, but maybe coming in and out of someone's life is easy for you, but for

there, you'll never be able to love me the way I need to be loved, and I'll never be able to accept the fact that he comes first.''

Her anger turned to sadness. "I'm sorry you didn't catch him, John. Really I am. But if you think I'm going to wait around indefinitely until you do, then you haven't learned a thing about me...or yourself, for that matter."

"But I did catch him."

Her look turned sharply skeptical. "I did," he insisted.

Rennie struggled to make sense out of what he was saying. It was only when she looked at him, *really* looked at him, that she saw what she'd been too angry and hurt to see before. There was an expression on his face that could only be described as peaceful. The tension was gone from his brow. There was no trace of anger in his dark eyes, no sign of the usual disillusion tugging the corners of his mouth into a frown. In the starkly handsome face that looked back at her, she saw only honesty.

"Did you—" She bit her lip, nervously anticipating his reply.

He shook his head and gave a fateful little shrug. "I couldn't do it. I couldn't kill him."

The revelation, coming so unexpectedly and so calmly, stunned Rennie. "You mean you let him go?"

"He's just like me, Rennie. He can't help being what he is. But that's where the similarity ends. He

but didn't. We have nothing to fear from him. It's over.''

Rennie melted into his arms that opened wide to receive her. A flutter caught in her throat, and in a breathy whisper she said, ''I'll stay. Tonight and forever.'' She drew his head toward hers and kissed him deeply, sealing her promise.

In this place of sunlight and shadow, filled with stark reality and steeped in mystery, Rennie's heart had found its home. This was where she belonged. This was her destiny.

While deep in the swamp, among a dwindling population, one big cat followed his own unique destiny.

* * * * *

This Mother's Day Give Your Mom A Royal Treat

Win a fabulous one-week vacation in Puerto Rico for you and your mother at the luxurious Inter-Continental San Juan Resort & Casino. The prize includes round trip airfare for two, breakfast daily and a mother and daughter day of beauty at the beachfront hotel's spa.

INTER·CONTINENTAL
San Juan
RESORT & CASINO

Here's all you have to do:

Tell us in 100 words or less how your mother helped with the romance in your life. It may be a story about your engagement, wedding or those boyfriends when you were a teenager or any other romantic advice from your mother. The entry will be judged based on its originality, emotionally compelling nature and sincerity. See official rules on following page.

Send your entry to:

Mother's Day Contest

In Canada
P.O. Box 637
Fort Erie, Ontario
L2A 5X3

In U.S.A.
P.O. Box 9076
3010 Walden Ave.
Buffalo, NY
14269-9076

Or enter online at www.eHarlequin.com

All entries must be postmarked by April 1, 2002. Winner will be announced May 1, 2002. Contest open to Canadian and U.S. residents who are 18 years of age and older. No purchase necessary to enter. Void where prohibited.

If you enjoyed what you just read,
then we've got an offer you can't resist!

Take 2 bestselling love stories FREE!

Plus get a FREE surprise gift!

Clip this page and mail it to Silhouette Reader Service™

IN U.S.A.
3010 Walden Ave.
P.O. Box 1867
Buffalo, N.Y. 14240-1867

IN CANADA
P.O. Box 609
Fort Erie, Ontario
L2A 5X3

YES! Please send me 2 free Silhouette Intimate Moments® novels and my free surprise gift. After receiving them, if I don't wish to receive anymore, I can return the shipping statement marked cancel. If I don't cancel, I will receive 6 brand-new novels every month, before they're available in stores! In the U.S.A., bill me at the bargain price of $3.80 plus 25¢ shipping and handling per book and applicable sales tax, if any*. In Canada, bill me at the bargain price of $4.21 plus 25¢ shipping and handling per book and applicable taxes**. That's the complete price and a savings of at least 10% off the cover prices—what a great deal! I understand that accepting the 2 free books and gift places me under no obligation ever to buy any books. I can always return a shipment and cancel at any time. Even if I never buy another book from Silhouette, the 2 free books and gift are mine to keep forever.

245 SEN DFNU
345 SEN DFNV

Name	(PLEASE PRINT)	
Address	Apt.#	
City	State/Prov.	Zip/Postal Code

 * Terms and prices subject to change without notice. Sales tax applicable in N.Y.
** Canadian residents will be charged applicable provincial taxes and GST.
   All orders subject to approval. Offer limited to one per household and not valid to
   current Silhouette Intimate Moments® subscribers.
   ® are registered trademarks of Harlequin Enterprises Limited.

INMOM01   ©1998 Harlequin Enterprises Limited

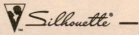

Silhouette® —

where love comes alive—online...

eHARLEQUIN.com

your romantic books

- ❤ Shop online! Visit Shop eHarlequin and discover a wide selection of new releases and classic favorites at great discounted prices.

- ❤ Read our daily and weekly Internet exclusive serials, and participate in our interactive novel in the reading room.

- ❤ Ever dreamed of being a writer? Enter your chapter for a chance to become a featured author in our Writing Round Robin novel.

your romantic magazine

- ❤ Check out our feature articles on dating, flirting and other important romance topics and get your daily love dose with tips on how to keep the romance alive every day.

- ❤ Learn what the stars have in store for you with our daily Passionscopes and weekly Erotiscopes.

- ❤ Get the latest scoop on your favorite royals in Royal Romance.

your community

- ❤ Have a Heart-to-Heart with other members about the latest books and meet your favorite authors.

- ❤ Discuss your romantic dilemma in the Tales from the Heart message board.

All this and more available at www.eHarlequin.com